TRACKS

"Wait!" Dave says. "What do you mean by tracks?"

"What I said. I told the authorities that in rural Oregon, east of Portland by a hundred miles, I looked down in the mud and saw fresh tracks of what seemed like some hooved animal. I wasn't dreaming!"

"And I saw a bird!" Dave says. "A few years ago . . ."

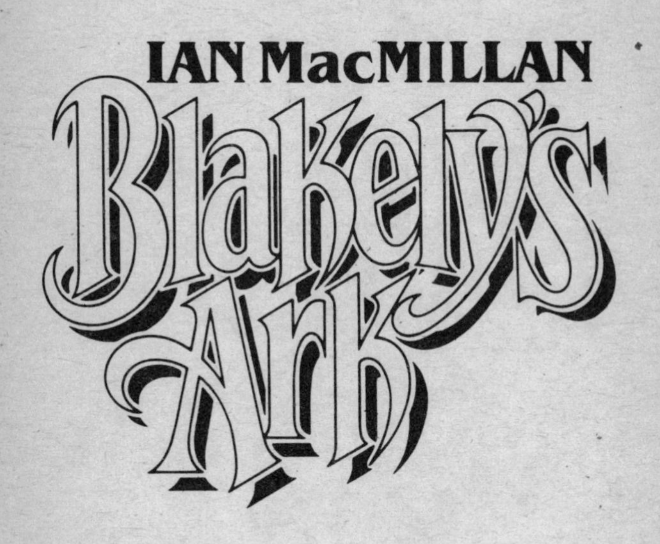

BERKLEY BOOKS, NEW YORK

BLAKELY'S ARK

A Berkley Book / published by arrangement with
the author

PRINTING HISTORY
Berkley edition / July 1981

For information address: Berkley Publishing Corporation,
200 Madison Avenue, New York, New York 10016.

ISBN: 0-425-04928-0

A BERKLEY BOOK ® TM 757,375

PRINTED IN THE UNITED STATES OF AMERICA

NAME
Parasitic Microencephalitis

ORIGINS
Unknown

CHARACTERISTICS
Virus capable of parasitic capacity on other viruses, probably adaptable in shape. Germination period—seven days. Infectious parasitic virus can be carried on breath, skin, lies dormant indefinitely, can travel through air great distances, infects through mucous membranes, is most virulent at time of victim's death.

SYMPTOMS
(in succeeding and/or simultaneous stages), headache, dizziness, nausea, vomiting, lowgrade fever, light and sound sensitivity, intolerable internal itching, various psychotic symptoms, loss of control of bodily functions, nervous prostration, convulsions, congestive heart failure, suffocation due to involuntary retching.

SURVIVAL RATE
None.

PREVENTION
No known successful techniques.

CURES
None.

Blakely's Ark

I

"Do *not* open the door. Do *not* open the door. Do *not* open the door," like that his father had said it, his face a swollen mask of agony in the broken study window, and the voice had so intense an emphasis that Dave knew he had to, just once. When he went into the house and passed the closed study door he felt light and airy with shock. The familiar small looseleaf notebook of instructions lay open to page 1 on top of the TV set, which Dave had never watched, and the instructions read:

1. *Make sure you have the passport case.*

Yes, right there. He opened it once, saw the corner of his lottery ticket peeking out of one of the slots.

2. *Apply the antibacterial jelly immediately.*

He glanced out the dining room window, saw the

desolate street running into town, lined by the remains of burned houses, and then rubbed the jelly on his face and arms, regardless of the common belief that it wouldn't help. How many millions had died despite it? In a burst of shaky laughter he updated an imaginary town border sign: New Florence, New York, population 4. And decreasing. If you were a warm blooded animal, even one of the last, it would still only be a matter of time. The jelly had an odd smell, of volatile gasses, fuel, camphor, and he kept at it now only because of the feverish intensity of his father's orders. Even dead his teacher seemed to watch, so Dave kept to the prescribed order of action with mechanical rigidity, his eyes beginning to flood with fear and his knees threatening to buckle.

3. *No matter how strong the impulse, even if the body is still moving, do not approach it.*

4. *Ignite house.*

He nodded, his vision warped by the flooding eyes, and began to laugh at the absurd terseness of number 4.

5. *On your way out pass by Marquand's for any messages he may wish to send with you.*

6. *Consult maps for route to Interchange and ramp for Buffalo entrance to Thruway.*

Dave sat down in the easy chair and put his hands on his face. Ignite house. Okay. But one look. Feeling the shame that comes with willing disobedience, he stepped to the study door and swallowed, and then noiselessly opened it to a one inch crack and held his breath. The narrow slit of a picture showed him the familiar form slumped on the desk over an open book, the oil lamp still on (peculiar—as the house erupted in flames the lamp would continue to weakly flicker). He moved slightly and shifted his strip of vision to a forearm cradling a tipped over can, the marijuana it would be, and in the ashtray he saw the little yellowed stubs. Dave closed the door and let out his breath. Somewhere on the desk there was the bottle which held the cyanide pills he probably took.

He went out the front door and to the garage, and sidling in alongside the car, which had been used last perhaps ten years ago, he grabbed the handlebars of the bicycle and wheeled it out. Then he went into the woodshed for the trailer, sleek and dull silver, once a reserve tank from a small plane, hand fashioned by his father for the journey. Inside were instructional manuals, medical books, dried foods, vacuum packed vitamins, woodsman's implements.

He had trouble hitching the trailer to the bicycle. His hands would not obey him. Finally he forced them to work, and was ready. Ignite house.

It was a matter of starting a couple of little fires inside, one in the living room and one in the kitchen. While the fires did their slow growing, he stood and looked around at the handmade means of lighting, the reclaimed woodstove, the hand pump installed through the kitchen floor. It seemed to him that most of his father's life since he had known him, now going on eighteen years, had amounted to two things, each done in sullen and drudging and relentless precision: staying alive at this house, and preparing Dave for the trip. 5. *On your way out pass by Marquand's—*

He stayed to watch the house fall, still seeing the strange picture of the lamp in the study flickering dimly against the advancing flames. It did not go as he expected: the foundation stood so long that it seemed foolish to stay and watch the flames gradually eat it away.

He went toward Marquand's via Center Street, the little trailer jerking annoyingly. The few houses left, overgrown with weeds and vines and vandalized years ago, passed out of his line of vision unrecognized because of their familiarity. The street ahead was littered with glass and rubble and burned out cars, and was partially obscured by the advancing weeds.

He stood forty feet away and shouted. The Marquands, seeing the little trailer, understood immediately. Mrs. Marquand mumbled sympathetically while her husband stood behind her, shotgun in hand, still adhering to the old caution. "So Charlie bought it?" he shouted.

Christie sat on the porch swinging slowly, and Dave saw that she now had breasts.

"That's your house then?" Marquand said, stepping in front of his wife. Dave nodded. "The Ceph?"

"Yeah. Charlie wanted to know if there was any messages or anything you wanted to—"

"Nope. So he got the Ceph. How is what I'd like to know." He mumbled to his wife. On her skirt were two spots where she dried her hands. Christie went on swinging. "I mean, it's been over a year, and every one was burned, and so I'd like to know how—"

"My dad said it was the traveller."

Mrs. Marquand came out with a hoarse sob and disappeared into the house and Christie quickly stood up before the swing, which bumped her once on the backs of her knees.

"Now say that again Dave," Marquand said. "What traveller?"

"One week ago—a man going up to Canada or so he said."

Christie yelled "Maaa!" and ran into the house.

"When'd Charlie go?"

" 'smornin' ."

Marquand went into the house, and Dave stood and listened to the desperate sound of their voices as they quickly talked it out, figuring their chances.

Christie came back out and threw herself back on the swing and went at it furiously, kicking her legs out and watching Dave.

"Then you got it too," she called.

"I don't know. My Dad told me to go anyway—says if I go according to the book I'll be okay."

"What book?"

"No no. If I'm careful. And I got a book anyway. Got lots of them. Says if—"

"I'll bet you got it. You'll start dancin' any minute an' my Dad'll have to pop you."

"He said if we're the only ones left in town then we probly won't get it. He says that if you go according to—"

Mr. Marquand came out again, composed. "Ah, Dave. Dave. We'd like to wish you a safe trip—for Charlie's sake. I mean for all the work he did. I hope it works out. You got all your stuff?"

"Yeah, all packed up."

"I wish Christie could go with you, but, well, the lottery you know. Anyways," and he looked away toward the column of dark smoke coming up from the other side of town, "anyway, I hope you make it. That traveller was here too."

"How close did he get? Was there any wind?"

"Twenty feet maybe. No, no wind. I don't know. Listen, I'd just as soon you said we weren't here, okay? Tell 'em everybody's gone? Traveller said they don't think there's anybody left above the Jersey–New York line—an' he told us some stories that sounded—well, we'd just as soon—"

"Well, okay," Dave said. "Hey? About the Ceph? You're okay most likely. Charlie he invited the guy into the house. You know Charlie when there was somebody to talk to."

"The poor guy," Marquand said. "So he bought it."

"Yeah. Kinda thought it was finished, but—"

"Bye Dave," Christie said. "I hope you make it."
"By Christie, Mr. Marquand."
"Take it easy kid."

He was no more than two minutes away from Marquand's, pumping along and annoyed at the feeling of the jelly on his skin and aware of the column of smoke hovering behind his left shoulder, when he had to stop. He stood there straddling the bike and cried, feeling a nauseating self disgust at his lack of control. "You *god*damned *chick*en," he said. "You *god*damned *chick*en." And then he was calm. He was suddenly overcome with a funny inertia. Before him the littered street stretched off absolutely clear in his vision, objective and desolate, and his eyes seemed suddenly to capture its complete meaninglessness with pinpoint lucidity. The sobbing stopped as quickly as it had begun, and now he stood over the bike, the heels of his hands resting on the grips, and felt hollow, clean and neutralized. He cleared his throat, downshifted, and started up again.

The area he now passes through he knows, the burned out and overturned cars which had been for him places to play with friends who dropped off one by one all through his life, until the last year or two, when it was him alone who went out to smash the windows and burn out the interiors. The familiar macadam road, overgrown with weeds working their way inward toward the faded white line in the middle, stretches off into the green hills, snaking through the little valleys. The panorama appears to be made up of green pillows depressed in random fashion by a giant piece of frayed black electrical tape.

Then he rolls to a stop at the Eagle Creek Bridge. Beyond it is new country for him, a stretch of around seven hundred kilometers to his new home. He straddles the bike, looks back once, and then takes a deep breath. He has a funny feeling that everything is now too large for him and that all distances are too great, and that the tissues and bones which encase his heart and brain are too vulnerable for all this. But despite the feeling he whispers, "okay, okay," and puts the bike in gear.

In places it is as if no death had ever occurred, where houses and barns stand intact and the fields and woods are green and immaculate. He views the new country with numb objectivity, and only the threat of oncoming dusk scares him. Night might not be so bad though, because the air is clean, different from the periodic odors of death which he associates with his town, all the way back in his memory to those days when his father and the other men, in self defense, burned the houses of the dead so that the acrid odor of burning flesh came through the smells of burning wood and plastic. He can see Charlie now, see Marquand too, standing before the Roberts house while inside the family, close friends, howls and dances with the fever, and Marquand, despite Charlie's disapproval, shoots those who come into view, Nancy, staggering with her hands gripped over her mouth, the father on his hands and knees. Dave remembers distinctly his father finally saying, "Okay, it's quiet. Is it quiet? Yeah, it's quiet, it's quiet. It is quiet," and approaching the house with a rock and a torch while Marquand, trembling and swearing, aims at little Chuck Roberts, who has suddenly stumbled out onto the porch, five years old, wearing oversized blue jeans Dave recognizes as his own, a handmedown gift to the little boy. The slug from the shotgun folds him in half and slams him back inside the house. That night Dave stands in the kitchen wondering dully about being nine years old, and hears his father sobbing in the study, and it is hearing this sound, not seeing the day of fires, of corpses, of whole families being relieved of their flushfaced agony by flying bullets, of mammoth fires fouling the sky—it is the sound of his father's crying that makes him rubberlegged with fear, and he knows at that moment that there is no hope.

To fight off the morbid fright at now being truly alone in increasing darkness, he concentrates on the motions of setting up a camp. Out comes the sleeping bag, one can of Vienna sausages and a patty of wheat germ. Before eating, he takes a pair of underpants (Charlie packed too many of them anyway) and removes the dust caked and rancid antibacterial jelly from his face and hands. Then, snorting at the thought of having to go through all this nonsense, he casts a large tube of it off into the weeds and returns to the Vienna sausages and wheat germ. The jelly was intended for use only in heavy bacterial presence, and he has left that behind. Now, water. Charlie packed a case of sealed plastic bottles of distilled water in the trailer. *Do not drink any water that has not been boiled a full fifteen minutes, a full rolling boil.*

Sitting under a maple tree in the dying light he eats the soft sausages and the tasteless wheat germ patty. Although he has camped in the woods many times on Charlie's orders, he has always feared darkness. There is no danger because there are no people to come after his food nor are there any animals who could do him harm, except perhaps for biting insects—'*avoid being bitten by mosquitoes, stung by bees, etc., as this opens you to infection which can host the encephalitis.*' There seem to be no bugs, and all warm blooded animals are gone, but the fear of the dark gnaws at him with forceful subtlety. Tiny sounds, gentle wafts of unexpected breeze, the hint of the smell of death in the air—reason cannot nullify the suspicions, the breath halting tension brought on by these little bits of evidence.

He goes to the trailer and finds the plastic bag of marijuana his father placed inside. Dave does not smoke much—when he does it is always a matter of sacrificing his throat for the dreamy but strangely clearheaded period of giggling pleasure. He rolls clumsily, losing half of the contents intended for the paper into the weeds. He lights up and sits under the tree and waits for the fear to subside.

He remembers, half in dream. He was ten.

"I did see it."

"I told you it is not possible—you must've seen something else." Shaking his head with angry conviction.

"In the big woods—I swear. It went down first, and then it went up behind some trees. It was brown."

Now thinking, looking into a cloud of bluegray smoke exhaled into the space above him. Cigarettes from his ancient tobacco stash in the cellar. "Listen, if that was true— If you really— No. Nothin's alive! No warm blooded animal is alive!"

"Well *that* was. It *was*. It went down first, and then up."

"Maybe you dreamed it, something like that. Nothing's alive for almost ten years now." Still thinking. "The big woods? I suppose if there *was* anything it might be— Nah, you dreamed it."

"Who cares anyway—don't make no difference anyway."

It didn't. But he saw it, flying so fast that there was no chance to really see what it looked like. Swooped into a dip close to the ground and then up again without flapping its wings so that for a moment before going behind the trees it seemed to soar like a thrown stone in a graceful parabola, freeing itself and relaxing in its perfect trajectory.

* * *

Dawn. A thin mist hangs low over the tall grasses. Bright mare's tails streak the sky. Dave is cold, shivering inside the green quilted sleeping bag. He is hungry, and the trailer sits off behind the bicycle shining with tiny beads of dew so that its curved side has in it a rainbow. He looks around at the fields, the stone fences overgrown with broom, and the macadam road snaking off toward the Buffalo Interchange. Up ahead there is a white car facing his way, a Ford, one of the ones Charlie said looked like a man with a receding hairline, the dome of glass topped with a thin peninsula of metal.

He gets up and stretches and decides to check out the car. He needs to walk. The muscles in his legs are stiff and sore, and the heels of his hands are sore from carrying his upper body weight against the handgrips of the ten speed.

The car bobs in front of him with the rhythm of his walking. The fields glitter with dew, and there is that familiar absolute soundlessness everywhere, except for the occasional buzz of an insect. The car looms closer. The tires are flat, and he swallows, looking in. He has seen this before. In the back seat are the mummified remains of a man and a woman, their clothes glued to their brown leather skin, which is glued to their skeletons. They are almost hidden in tight veils of cobwebs. The man seems to have his arm around the woman, whose remains are drawn up in a position of sleeping on his shoulder. He has his head back on the speaker for the tape apparatus in the front. On the back and front floors there are thousands of dead flies, perhaps three inches deep, the host for their reproduction abundant but their food scarce. The glove compartment is open, meaning the car was probably pilfered for its valuables, probably ten years ago around the Second Wave by some idiot who most likely survived only a week and a half after looking inside.

Back at the bike he eats quickly, gulps water, and throws the container into the weeds, thinking that slowly but surely the weight of the trailer will decrease. He packs his gear hastily and gets ready to mount up. Then, chuckling softly, he finds a nice three pound rock, and mounting the bike he holds it up at shoulder level. As he passes the white Ford he gently lobs the rock at the glass dome and rides on. It does not break, but instantly there appear around the stone's dent a million minute cracks, enfolding the two lovers behind a glittering curtain. And he thinks: goodbye dead folks, germs, goodbye fires and guns and death. Ahead is the Complex, living people, voices. In the last week, suspecting that his time had come, he thought frequently about that moment, that first conversation, that strange freedom to walk right up to a person without fear of infection. Would there be a gate of some kind? Some kind of a ceremony at his entrance? All of his life he had seen pictures of the Complex, had heard stories about the strange freedom to walk in its sterile atmosphere—gleaming pavilions, zoos, swimming pools, the freedom to accidentally rub shoulders with another human, with millions of them, all under the huge dome. And Charlie, whose flesh still cooks in the smoldering remains of the house? He would not witness this. His life ended in caution—for years, even with his own son, he harbored deep suspicions of infection. They had maintained a body's length distance and had become used to it.

New Information: this recent addition to the looseleaf notebook meant nothing to him until his father, drawn and puff eyed, told him to go into the woods with adequate provisions for longer than he had ever camped before. Seven days—the period of germination. Had the time come? He rode his bike north to look for car windows to break, houses and barns to burn or explore, but cautiously, *'avoid (ing) enclosures, damp areas, barns in which manure, no matter old, is piled, locked houses, cars.'* Voluptuous billows of black smoke marked his explorations. He set up camp by night and fought the boredom. He would spend hours sitting in a single position, rocking, eyes closed, softly moaning the time away, still in a state of gape-mouthed shock at the vision of his father. Stay away, twenty feet at least. He now recognized the obvious mistake he had made (he even shook hands with the man, making Dave shake his head in amazement at this incredible breach of caution). "But you don't understand," he had said, "I mean since you haven't known that many people, then maybe solitude is okay for you, but this guy, this guy was at Columbia when I was! Can you imagine?" All this said in apologetic amazement. Anybody else could be that careless, but not Charlie. "Go quick," he said, "and we'll see. In a week there'll be nothing to worry about." But they both knew—a traveller, hundreds of miles from the Complex, the circumstances, it finally dawned on them, were too suspicious.

New information: it was more important now that the time had come, the only addition in the last four or five years, including the status of the lottery, the condition of the Complex, the problems involved in getting safely to it.

Yes, when he returned, again stopping within twenty feet of the house, he realized the gravity of his father's error. The traveler had been infected. A chance in a thousand, but infected. The sounds of Charlie's agony came from the study—he was shouting with shock and amazement. From what Dave had observed about the disease he was walking in circles, probably holding his head, periodically vomiting, his balance, reason, control, ebbing away and capitulating to symptoms described as a searing itch, an incredible, almost heatless fever, a madness produced by the effects of virulent parasitic microencephalitis. Dave yelled, "Charlie! Charlie, what's wrong!" and the face, purple with apparent rage, appeared behind the window and the palms of the hands were against the sides of his head, pulling the face into a grotesque mask, like someone trying brutally to imitate an Oriental. Then he made a few exasperated hand gestures, almost as if he didn't want to because they distracted him from his indulgence in his agony: they said, go to the Complex, the trailer is prepared. He tottered, and his head broke the window out, and so the rest came in a strained shout—"I sprayed the house so you can come in for the passport case and the book oh *god* I—pick up the book. There's new stuff in it—" and all the time Dave stood listening in rubberlegged disbelief. "Hurry, hurry! Dave, I—I can't hold much longer! Do what the book says, and the study! Do *not* open the door. Do *not* open the door. Do *not* open the door!" and then he fell back over something, as if the power of the final throat ripping scream after his last order created momentum, almost like a rocket. It was then that he must have taken the cyanide for fear of becoming unreasonable enough to come out of the study.

And as he pumps along he still does not worry about the new information in the book. In a way he looks forward to it as a preface to that first meeting with new people. About the rest of the book's contents—he had long ago become bored to the point of exasperation about his father's meticulous preparations for the trip, the multitude of warnings, which had by now been imbedded in his mind like some meaningless system of prayers familiar to one longsince without faith. Dave had always argued that it seemed like too much preparation for one little trip to the Complex, and Charlie had always countered by saying you could never tell what you'd run into or how long it would take to be admitted or even *if* you'd be admitted.

The new information is not important until he emerges from the narrow macadam road and is shaken to a halt by this panorama: perhaps seventy meters wide, maybe more, shining black with white lines sweeping along it defining its incredible grace and size, shooting off into the hot, midday distance in a mammoth curve that extends maybe fifteen kilometers, in complete interruption and subjugation of the slovenly woods and fields on either side, is the Thruway. The vision staggers him. The black and white perfection of the highway is too much, its untainted might, lying there baking in the sun like some invulnerable and self-indulgent serpent, seems to him a dream. Could anything survive, maintain its wholeness when the screaming populations of cities and towns danced out their agonies more than a decade ago? Could anything in the world remain so unscathed?

Off to his right he sees the burned out remains of what must be the outskirts of Buffalo, blackened towers, buildings whose lower floors are choked with vines, here and there a burned out car. He stretches, looking back at the highway. All the way, he thinks. I will ride that all the way. He must now consult the new information.

The passport case and the notebook are in a small bag mounted on the frame of the bicycle. He sits and opens the case. There he sees his birth certificate and the certificate of the lottery confirming his registry number from the old tax rolls. The certificate itself is something like the old money his father used to show him: beautifully engraved in grey and green, with strange symbols, eagles holding arrows, the number in red, the little strip of pure silver running through the registry number (Hunter, David T. jo32851-662

He knows it by heart). In the center is a picture of John F. Kennedy (1917-1963), one of the old presidents. 'Entitles the Qualified Bearer to Free and Lawful Entry into Controlled Atmosphere Complex, New York, New York. Not Transferrable.' On the bottom, in minute and meticulous lettering: Bureau of Printing and Engraving, Washington, D. C.

The notebook: 'Dave—I am told by Mr. Celetti that things have degenerated since we last heard of the Complex. The structure itself is intact, invulnerable, Celetti says, but getting to it is another matter.

Use the original maps. Go through Syracuse toward Albany. Do not follow the thruway all the way. Instead, get off at Utica and approach the Complex from a more westward direction (see attached routes).

The reason for the route change is that the population immediately outside the Complex has diminished to about ten million (he says), and you may regard the population surrounding the Complex as a system of concentric circles. Nearest the Complex is a relatively stable society which has managed, through means too numerous to mention here, to slow down the rapid decline of its numbers by means of a faultless system of disposal of the dead, new medicines put in food, and a working system of personal isolation. These people, Celetti says, have also managed to get short periods of electrical power mostly for purposes of entertainment and for medical purposes.

The next ring outside the above is made up of less fortunate people who seem to have no stable system of organization, no hygenic means of disposal of the dead (they burn, as we did, but without dealing with still infected inner remains, which become sources of new infection through flies and so forth). Celetti says that here there is a lot of crime and frequent local outbreaks of the Ceph., especially in the summer.

The last ring? A sparsely populated area dominated he says by vicious adolescents, mostly orphans. He has told me stories which I hate to contemplate when I think of you attempting to pass through the areas controlled by these people. Why the savagery? In the middle ring, or which these young people are offshoots, the average life span is now 24–26 years, which would make the final ring outside more easily explainable. They have lost all hope of survival and don't care.

Note: the worst thing about this is that those closest to the Complex in the inner ring and those who hence have more hope have fenced themselves off from the second ring population and defend their boundaries with whatever means are necessary. They consider themselves the only legitimate population outside the Complex. I am told that they use guns, gasses of various sorts, and so on. Those less fortunate in the middle ring use whatever means they can to eliminate the younger bandits on the outside.

Now, getting through: travelling by major highways means certain death. If you approach through the once densely populated area of northern New Jersey, you can do it without being seen. The Thruway is wide open space, but in New Jersey, working through smalltown streets, you can make it to the middle ring, where your lottery certificate *should* give you legal right to pass. The routes are marked out in the new maps. Be careful though. He says if someone manages to steal all your stuff he will probably also try to take your index fingers (no kidding) and use some means to 'wear' the skin on entry to the Complex. It is not likely that this will happen any more, but it used to with some frequency.

The Ceph. There has not been a major outbreak in eleven months, which seems like a record compared to the old days. Of course, take all the usual precautions upon approaching any area where there are likely to be people.

Dave—remember the story I told you about the mousetraps and the pingpong balls? Where a room full of set traps each with a ball on the snapper was fine until the man threw in an extra ball, at which the whole room exploded with flying balls and traps? Remember that as long as you live. Wherever you are, one infected person, that last ball, may at any moment be falling toward the quiet traps all set with balls on their triggers. You must remember that close contact with anyone infected means certain death. If I could only get across to you how bad I feel about that traveller. I have a funny, ominous feeling right now while I write this. But then, if he manages to get this far, how could he be infected? If he is, then all I can say is I know you are prepared. I know you are tough and have something the rest of them don't have—a method of fulfilling the instinct for survival. Who knows? Maybe you'll never have to use it. But it's the only legacy I figure is worth anything these days.'

The writing stops there. Dave closes the notebook and looks at the Thruway again. He sighs, thinking of Charlie, and then flips the book open to a familiar page: '*—should become necessary to defend yourself against the approach of infected persons, grit your teeth and use the new hunting bow. Use a hunting arrow rather than a target arrow. Be sure to open the bow carefully—until it is latched, the hinge built into the handle is not that strong. And practice when you get the chance.*'

He remembers: "Try again."

He draws back, aiming, sighting along the shaft.

"Don't let your wrist bend—you'll twang yourself."

The index finger of the hand pulling the string back brushes along his lip and gently hooks into the corner of his mouth. He lets off. Charlie watches, smiles with satisfaction.

"Jesus, hardly believe it." He muses. "Parallax correction," he says. "It's a sixth sense."

"What is it?"

"You correct your own displacement in aiming—but you don't have to know it—you got it by instinct." He points at the target. "You also got the bloop correction. Amazing."

Dave sees dusk advancing upon him and gets out his sleeping bag and food. Down among the bottles of water and medical books and bike tools he sees part of the smooth handle of the bow, and next to it the quiver, containing twenty-two fine arrows, eighteen hunting and four target. He looks up at the immense and peaceful stretch of highway and thinks, that will be smooth.

The fear of the darkness: he lies there in the bag and looks off toward the ink blackness of the space under which lies the highway, his eyes wide open even though he is tired. He lies waiting for the groping touch of something, some vice-like grip, perhaps on the back of the neck. It will be one of the unlucky dead, one of the multitude of insane and agonized even in death, groping in mindless pain through the darkness jealously searching out those lucky enough to survive the last wave. He even believes that his mother, dead since he was six, stalks somewhere in her melancholy and greyhaired pain, not knowing that her next victim is her own son—she cannot know by feeling someone who is three times larger than when she last saw him, standing off thirty feet away crying while she permits herself to be tied to a chair by Charlie who is wrapped in an army issue plastic suit, and she sits, looks through her bloodshot eyes and tries to perceive through her clawing agony, through the loss of sense and balance, the little boy who is not allowed to approach. And when she vomits into her lap she still seems to look in his direction, Dave the lucky fugitive from the inevitable Ceph. And now, stalking nearby in the weeds, glumly searching for one of the few remaining alive, she chances upon a form hunched in a sleeping bag, and in lustful curiosity stumbles, her face twisted in pain, toward the form, to wrench it into her lonely world, to choke, decapitate, disembowel, burn the form into her world, to do something to ease the endless melancholy of being one of the unlucky dead.

He gropes out of the bag, his knees weak and his heart high in his chest, and approaches the trailer, trying to remember where he put the marijuana.

Pumping along at middle speed, he runs the wheels of the bicycle on the immense dotted line of his choice of one lane of the Thruway, so that the soft sound comes at him with deadening regularity: ba-blip ba-blip ba-blip. Two sounds for the tires hitting the thick paint and two for the subtle bouncing down to the macadam. He is trying to remain calm in the suspicious recognition that he feels unaccountably tired and weak. He is three days out and it is too soon to be feeling the effects of an infection yet, but still he feels some subtle symptom is at work. He smells funny, too—a mixture of skin oil and sweat and anti-bacterial jelly, all gone peculiarly rancid.

But it could be the other: the strange feeling Charlie would call depression. Dave identifies it as feeling like nothing, as if he has no matter, no real substance. With each mile between his burned house and his destination he feels a kind of decrease in weight, as if he is closer to death than ever, even closer than that time when he began to pay no attention to the bodies of the people of his town strewn about. Ba-blip ba-blip ba-blip.

If only that foul idiot, that cruel son of a bitch of a

traveller had not appeared to steal one of the living to accompany him into death. That is it: the dying are jealous and will do anything to deny life to the lucky fugitives. To them the living are like water to a thirsty man and they must drink them in until their jealous lust is satisfied. He could see the man's face twisted into a simpering grin betraying the obvious fact that in knowing he was dead he had chucked all pity for the living. The man walked right up to Charlie! Dave wouldn't even do that. There was no compromising the maintenance of their six foot buffer zone of safety, even when they played monopoly, half-consciously keeping their distance. At those rare times when Dave suddenly smelled in the breeze the pungent odor of his father's sweat, he would automatically move to a cross wind position. And the traveller—it was clear that he wanted to get close to smear the viscous oils of his infection on the hand of Charlie, who, surprised that the man would so readily approach, did not recognize that he was being murdered by the heartless bastard. That was Charlie—he could be fooled, deceived by the conventions of his old experience. Dave, still a baby at the outbreak of the first wave, where ninety million people died, could never be fooled.

He remembers: he is twelve, hiding behind a bush. Charlie is tinkering with irrigation troughs. Hunched over his boards he saws away in an even shash shash, the faded hump on the back of his blue workshirt the highest point of his body. Laughing, Dave bursts from the bushes yelling, Charlie! Charlie! running toward him so that he drops the saw. What? What?

Dave stops in his tracks panting, his face twisted with surprise, and says softly, nothin'

Charlie bursts out laughing, says, you *got* me. You *got* me. My God I thought you'd never be able to— And they go inside and drink water. This is the last time the game is played. It had begun when Dave was about six, a ridiculous game used to occupy the space of the boredom, which, like distance, had become one of the characteristic conditions of their lives. Charlie started by saying to Dave, Hey Dave? Dave would say, what? Charlie would say, nothin' and chuckle to himself and go on about his business. For years they went at it, trying to catch each other, until the game had become so sophisticated that either of them would go to great lengths to achieve the dupe.

Some towns appear from a distance to have survived the first and second waves: there houses are burned out, and near one he sees the fenced area of pits meant for disposal of the dead. Other towns appear to have been obliterated by the first wave, and therefore are without damage. It is because of the monotony that he decides to venture down one of the ramps and take a closer look. The town is on the outskirts of Syracuse, and he is jarred out of the peaceful monotony of the Thruway by the roughness of the old macadam. It takes five minutes of passing the bramble hidden houses before he enters the main street. Here the cement has interrupted the advance of the high weeds. The stores are still intact. Western Auto, with its array of shining auto parts. A drugstore with its door broken in. The same for all food stores. They have been emptied. He stops the bike in front of the bookshop. On one side of the bookshop is the emptied liquor store and on the other is a large house with thick white pillars going up two storeys and high bramble on the front lawn.

He finds a stone and smashes the glass door of the bookshop and steps through, cautiously avoiding the jagged pieces of glass still clinging in the door edges. The books, some cobwebbed into obscurity, stand ranked according to size and subject. There are the various treatises, descriptions, color brochures free from the U. S. Government, spread out on a table, one about the proposed complex ('proposed' meaning that this town went with the second wave), one dull looking booklet with small print explaining the lottery laws, which he has seen, and the President's Report on the Status of the Population, which he has seen.

He shrugs and leaves. Nothing new. He works his way through the weeds to the pillared house. There is always a moment of ghostly insecurity when he goes into one of these houses, as if the spirits of the dead inside could somehow infect him, yet he is curious. The front door is open and he steps inside, immediately smelling the familiar musty odor of mummified remains. He is probably the first person to enter this house in over a decade, but inside he sees that it has once been ransacked—the liquor cabinet is cleaned out, and across the beautiful oriental rug is a hallway littered with cardboard boxes, probably cereals and flour and the like, rejected by the looters of so long ago because of the chance of infection connected with any grain product, anything that could grow mildew or molds. In the dining room he finds a *Time* magazine, a later issue than he has ever seen. "Now *that's* something," he says. Evidently the owner of the house or the looters had been south before dying and had picked it up. Charlie had told him many times about the circulation of information, how the range decreased wave by wave. Even though the magazine was printed when Dave was a kid, it would be interesting to read. On the cover there is a large black and white grainy picture of a blob, with a small egg implanted on its side. The caption: "Dr. Lewisohn's Discovery—Adaptive Shape." In the corner, "*Time* offers this issue without charge as a public service."

Dave rolls the magazine up and puts it in his back pocket, and heads for the kitchen. There, before an open freezer door, the lower portion of a combination freezer-refrigerator, lie the remains of a baby, its small skeleton cobwebbed heavily, remnants of a diaper one with the skeleton. The shell of a whole lobster faces the small skull. It was apparently all the starving baby could find, and unable to do anything with it, the baby died right there. As he has noticed before, the skulls of the very young have a neat, diamond shaped hole on top.

Syracuse: the Thruway goes almost above it, sweeps over the black streets choked with abandoned cars and trucks, here and there a skeleton, streams unaffected past the immense buildings in their glassed perfection and their awesome bulk, all grouped closely. Here and there along the Thruway cars are parked on shoulders, some of them with remains inside, and Dave pumps hard at the bike to leave the place and get back to the countryside. The city scares him because of its cement and metal density. The wind in the buildings is like a voice, a soft chorus. He is relieved that the Thruway seems to pass without making contact, even though the vast, blank faces of the buildings slowly loom less than a hundred meters from him. In a half hour the buildings diminish in size, like a set of stairs descending, until the Thruway dips back toward the earth, toward the weed-choked and shingletopped houses and finally open space.

The heat of the day boils off the macadam. His progress seems excruciatingly slow, he floats through a monotonous silence broken only by the persistent hiss of the tires, and the forgotten jerk of the trailer hitch. The rhythm of riding the bike has become as unnoticed as a heartbeat in the half dazed perception of panorama passing slowly out of his vision, his fatigued legs give in to the exhaustion they know lies just beyond the slightest increase in effort, and can no longer be duped into impetuous exertion.

The Thruway sweeps through Utica, suspended on

pillars so that Dave floats slowly past the mute planes of the buildings. Then it dips again, signifying the outskirts and the opening out to fields.

Glass shattering, pieces falling on cement: so unmistakable that he pulls the bike up and waits. "People," he whispers. Sixty meters away, so close that he is locked straddling the bike in an inertia of wariness. Utica is too far up for these people to be of the outer ring. This is at least three hundred kilometers outside of that. Now he hears nothing, and that scares him more.

(It is one of those edge of town streets, once bustling with the selling of cars and the pumping of gas, and over there a bowling alley. The sounds came from a little group of stores disappearing around a corner on a street that marked the end of the shopping part of town and the beginning of the residential part, houses with weedchoked lawns and here and there the remains of people, those on lawns fertilizer for green and verdant weeds.)

He must leave, but he does not. A kind of infection has his curiosity, and he wants to at least see from a distance the only other human beings he has seen in years besides the Marquands, Charlie, and the infected traveller.

He decides to be more cautious than he thinks is necessary. He straps on the little leather pouch in which are his birth certificate and his lottery certificate, and unhitches the trailer from the bike. Then he gingerly slides his bow and quiver of arrows out of the trailer, wincing as he rattles cans and packages of dried foods. He opens the bow, feeling its hinge resist in its saturation with the heavy oil, and straightens it to a loud click. He passes the bow behind his knee, puts one end on the toe of his boot and pulls the other end from behind his shoulder to loop the heavy waxed string into position. The wood of the handle, smooth as a polished statue, lies snugly in his hand.

The exit ramp is a hundred meters ahead, and he quickly skims down it, surprised at the bike's manageability. Once on the lumpy macadam, he rides back toward the origin of the sounds, the string of the bow comfortably bound against his chest and the quiver light against his back. He stops. Over in front of a bar guarded for all eternity by a skeleton partly propped against the marble half wall below the window, skull in lap of bones, are four bicycles and rucksacks.

"—creeeeem fucking sherry!" someone shouts.

"eeeEEEEHA!"

The owner of one of the voices emerges, looks around, and suddenly stands at attention. Dave waves. They are separated by forty meters of rubble littered macadam. The guy looks back into the bar and speaks softly, and the others emerge. They are big, older than Dave, all wearing denim and green army jackets like Charlie wore in fall and spring.

"Hey chief!" the first one yells.

"Hi—what are you doing up this far?"

"What are *you* doing?" More hushed conversation.

"I'm from up north—goin' to the Complex," Dave says. "Where you from?"

"Acapulco," the first says, and they all laugh. "Just blew in on a humpin' jet. Where're your friends?"

"No," Dave says, "I'm serious—up north. Been there all this time. No friends. I'm alone."

"Nobody alive up there Jack. You infected or something?"

"Nope, you?"

"Sure, we all are." One goes into a parody of a death dance, sliding along the wall and wailing and shaking his fists, retching loudly. "Come have some cream sherry with us—nobody sick here. Where'd you really come from?"

"North I said. Others live up there too. No kidding. Once I even saw a bird."

For some reason this draws laughter from all of them. The death dance one says, "Hey, there's a bird in them there hills—goddammit boys, what're we doin' with this sherry shit? Let's find the bird!" More laughter.

Number One seems to be thinking, scratching his head and wincing with concentration. Then he says, "Men, we've got to check this out! Say, stranger, this bird, did he say anything to you?"

"Well I did see one," Dave says. "I'm just passin' through. What is the condition of the Complex?"

"Complex? What Complex? Oh, *that* Complex. It turned into a balloon and went up in the air," Number One says in mock surprise, a studious, questioning look on his face, "and left a big hole in the ground? And you know what we found in the hole? Really? A sausage about a thousand feet long!"

"No really," Dave says, laughing with the others.

"And my question is what was the sausage doing there?"

Death Dance rummages in his rucksack. Then, while Dave screws his face up with humorous curiosity, the guy drops on one knee, hunches his head down, almost like someone in prayer. A puff of grey smoke, a shallow crack, and zing something goes off the brick wall just above Dave's head so that a shower of grains falls into his hair. It takes him a full three seconds before he realizes he has been shot at. Death Dance comes up from the pistol and looks.

"He always misses," Number One says.

Dave backs along the wall to a doorway and peers around. There are only two left at the bar door. The others have gone. Dave snorts and takes out his bow and a target arrow, sets it, stands out on the sidewalk. He draws the shaft over the felt rider all the way back so that he gently hooks his index finger into the corner of his mouth, and places the point of his estimated parallax correction at the wooden door between the two guys, and lets off. A little high—it whangs into the top door sill.

"Hey, now you put that twangy fucker down."

"Tell him to put his little whatchacallit away then."

"Ooee!" Death Dance says, "*Dead*ly *Dud*ley."

There is more hushed conversation. Now Dave realizes he should be off, that this foolishness has run its course. And he has wasted an arrow. "Hey, can you tell me anything about what's happening down there? C'mon, what're you doin' up here?"

"Well," Number One says, "sheeit, I'll tell you. Ain't no place where a feller c'n jack off without bein' caught at it. I mean Tex it's a pain in the *out* house."

"Where are your other friends? Lemme talk to them."

"They're around behind you somewhere, shithead. Probably looking for your gear. We're hungry." Dave looks around, cocks his head to listen. "Forget it," Number One says, "they're already up there on the highway eating right now. Boy you are a dumb fuck."

"Looting is a capital offence!" Dave yells. "You can't. The Martial Law says—"

They cackled at the Martial Law.

"Yoo-hoo!" From behind him. They have his trailer. One guy holds cans in the air. "Put your bibbies on and say grace, hungry campers!"

"Hey put that down!" He knows it is useless. Once touched, it might as well be contaminated. He storms toward them in an almost childlike fury, clumsily trying to root a hunting arrow. Another hollow crack. He turns back to the others and sees Death Dance aim again. Another puff, this time hitting leaves behind him.

"All right," he says, and aims, draws all the way back, hooks his index finger and lets off. And in the soft and hollow space of time of the arrow in flight (in its graceful and almost bloopless arc, flat for half the distance and then pulled soaring slightly lower, the shaft spinning) he watches in disbelief at its almost comic accuracy, and sees it place Death Dance on his rump and then ease him back so that his head hits the pavement with a trivial pop.

Dave's legs can hardly hold him, and he looks down at the bow openmouthed as Number One jumps away from the writhing form of Death Dance. One then edges in and with his foot brings the gun toward himself and picks it up. "Aww poor Hankie!" he says, "hey, what's Hankie's last name?"

"Who the hell knows?" one of the others yells.

"Poor Hankie Whonose—dominoes and biscuits forever amen."

Dave gets out another hunting arrow.

Number One waves the other two away, and they disappear behind a house. Then Number One shoots Death Dance in the head, awkwardly, holding the pistol upside-down, his face screwed up in experimental concentration. Death Dance draws up around himself and relaxes. The other two show up at the bar door, and they hastily pack up their gear and leave, taking with them the fourth rucksack and the food pilfered from Dave's trailer. They pay no attention to Death Dance.

"Okay," Number One says, mounting his bicycle, "we'll catch you another time, fuckface."

"Yeah, same to you," Dave mutters softly.

He stands gazing across the macadam at the form lying on the sidewalk, the arrow pointing its feathers straight into the air. He holds back the vague impulse to walk over to look—*do not approach the body*. He walks the bicycle back toward the highway ramp, seeing ahead the trailer he can no longer touch. Then he stops, in front of a trim, two-story house. He fumbles in his pocket for the little wooden box and heads for the front door, which is open. He looks in, sees no remains, and under an easy chair sees an old magazine, which he opens and squashes into wads. He strikes a match and sets fire to the paper, goes back outside, carefully closing the door behind him.

And riding slowly, hearing the first crackling of the fire, he thinks, so that's what they're like. He passes the little silver trailer. Food, books, water. All gone. Lucky he put the papers in the bike bag. Again the rigidity with which he had been taught to honor the code of caution keeps him from going to reclaim what has been only briefly touched by hands most likely not infected. Yet there is that chance. In a few days the three of them could be dead. He shifts gears and moves on. As he leaves, there will at least be the oddly comforting column of smoke behind him.

Inside of an hour he goes shopping, as Charlie would have put it. It is a matter of climbing through the broken window of a hardware store and collecting up a few objects: a pot for boiling water, canteen for carrying it, matches, one deflated backpack and a cheap knife (the other 'shoppers' years back took the better stuff, the red-handled Swiss knives and the class backpacks). The only real luck he has is in finding a good sleeping bag.

Food is another problem. He knows that, less than 300 kilometers from the Complex, he will need little, but Charlie always told him that you had to have extra rations regardless. He will have to break into the houses of the dead, not in Utica but in some town that went with the first wave. So it is down Route 28 now, skimming along the macadam, to look for a clean town. He rides light, frequently looking back at the smoke rising straight into the windless sky. His eyes dart into the limits of his peripheral vision. He is excited and optimistically wary.

Richfield Springs is a museum of life before the Ceph. Beautiful nineteenth century houses lined along mapleshaded streets, some with cars parked in driveways, here and there strangely delicate evidence of the serenity of the past: a swing hanging from the branch of a tree, a rusted tricycle on a porch, and on another a folded newspaper. No houses are burned. Only the town center has been looted. There, at the crossroads of two rural highways, there are skeletons, burned cars, bits of evidence of violence and agony. But off on the side streets among the huge houses it is as if nothing has happened to alter anyone's life. Dave stops the bike and as he had done as a small child holds the flat of his hand against his nose to block the weeds on the front lawns from his vision and imagines under his index finger lawns sparkling with sprinklers, children, verdant grass mowed close to the earth.

He breaks into twelve houses before finding anything of use. Before evacuating, this family took its food but neglected four packages of dehydrated chicken noodle soup. According to Charlie it would be all right providing you could stand the flat taste, providing each package was closely examined to see if air tightness held, and providing the water was boiled fifteen minutes. An even better discovery: behind the house next door he finds sweet potato vines—the deep green leaves, he learned from Charlie, are edible and packed with vitamins. As usual, in half of the houses he must pass remains, which he does not look at for more than a second. It seems that it was commonplace for the dying in Richfield Springs to have wine accompany them into death. Dust caked bottles appear nearby skeletons.

The *Time* magazine, which he had placed in his bike bag before running into the guys in Utica. He sits in the vapor of boiling water before his fire and reads small exerpts:

From "A Perspective on Dr. Lewisohn's Discovery", "—phenomenon of transference of host making the use of such drugs as D-4 and Penicillin derivatives useless. These drugs have too narrow a range of effect on the great variety of germs that can bring up even the most minor infection in the body. The FDA Emergency Research Force has nearly cured a case or two, but at such great cost and labor that it will never be feasable to treat the disease. We must come up with drugs that affect the parasitic virus itself—so far we can find nothing. Worse, there is a chance that the invention of a super drug to kill a super virus might produce a super-super virus."

From "Transition" (A list of perhaps three hundred names, persons of note whose lives have been claimed by the Ceph.):

Abbott, Henry E., 1920, Speaker of the House of—

Abelard, Joseph H., 1956, Special Counsel to the Emergency Session of—

Agaard, Martin G., 1936, Colorful Senator from—

From a pictorial article on progress in construction of the Controlled Atmosphere Complex: Photograph from the air, making it look like a grey and pockmarked flower, each petal a new extension, or, like the growth of caterpillars outward from a center section by section. A photograph of the inside—it is bright, with suspended walkways, people strolling, conversing as if the sky were infinite. On the right, some kind of a railway with cars hanging from the bottom. A photograph of a typical residence unit.

Compact but with the suggestion of space. The furniture is made of plastic. Plants hang around. The people smile, enjoy physical closeness. Another photograph of a globe in which animals graze. Dave recognizes a Giraffe and a Zebra. Attendants watch. Off in the background, he sees men in shorts playing tennis. Thinking, my God, I'll get up and go to the zoo, maybe ride that train thing. I'll meet someone somewhere and we might try playing tennis. Maybe there will be some girl who will watch from the edge of the zoo. We might sit someplace and eat and talk.

From "The Source" "—apparent simultaneous emergence in five different places in three continents rules out the idea of the 'long dormant virus' reappearing after millions of years. That, Lewisohn believed, was too coincidental. He remains convinced that we created it—"

Dave briefly scans an article about U.S.-U.S.S.R. agreements to trade treatment findings, U.S.-U.S.S.R. agreements to keep open communications via defense and nuclear armament control. Agreements of same to experiment with oceanic mini-complexes, using nuclear submarines as bases.

More photographs, these of solar converters mounted on the Complex.

Finally, an appendix to the magazine entitled "A Survival Handbook—Means of Avoiding Exposure, Preparing Food, Treating Minor Injuries."

This Dave will read, but not now. The fire crackles, the soup and potato greens will be ready shortly. He wonders if what he smells in the vapor is chicken.

Lying in the darkness, zipped comfortably in his bag, he knows why he feels no fear. With his fingers intertwined under his head he stares wide-eyed at the black, cloudless sky dappled with the little points of stars and feels a strangely familiar kind of neutralization. He had created a corpse, and there is something about it that makes him calm. It is not a good feeling or a bad feeling. A feeling without tone.

He remembers: it is during one wave or another, he can no longer identify them by number. In fact, by the time they got to the fourth, there wasn't anybody around to worry about numbers any more. The days are paced with the sounds of fires, shots, screams. Charlie is out again burning houses and trying to keep order, trying to separate the clean from the infected. Dave sneaks out north of town into the fields where he will meet some of his friends. Ronald Castle is the chief of the little group. He is twelve, Dave and the others around nine. While playing in the trees they see old Rob Mossman lumber into the woods, his eyes red and bleary, his balance gone, his mouth open and producing a sustained moan. He stops to retch near a tree, coughs up a little yellow string of mucous. He is going somewhere to die, staggering along, his head almost below the slight hump of his back crossed by the faded straps of his overalls. Finally he sits down as if pushed from the front. The boys come down out of the trees and regroup upwind of him, all knowing the rules. Rob Mossman rocks slowly, his eyes and nose running. He is in the last stages—madness, they know, is next. They know he can rise again and stagger on to infect others. Ronald Castle says we gotta kill him—we gotta stop him. Get some stones quick, and in a silent flurry of action the boys search around for their stones. Castle watches Mossman, permitting only quick glances behind him. Then he takes a rock from a kid and approaches on tiptoe and Mossman turns and through his burning eyes perceives the boy—he raises his hand as if to speak and comes out with a garbled three word command. Castle is a sidearm thrower and misses the first time. Bravely he steps closer. Dave stands, rock in hand, waiting for

Castle's command. Another sidearm throw smacks Mossman on the neck, and he bellows at the sky. Castle says, okay, come up, and the smaller boys approach, dangerously close, Dave thinks, and begin hurling the stones. Dave watches only his own throws, and his third pops Mossman on the kneecap, and he giggles with rubberlegged mischief. I got him, he says, his voice quaking. Hey, I got him. The others pay no attention. They watch their own throws. It takes them a long time to pelt the old man over on his side. Castle notices the wind pick up behind them and approaches to within seven feet. From there he works on the old man with his sidearm throws until it is apparent that he is dead. Next they gather leaves, twigs and branches to burn the body. It is a ritual they have all observed before and they act without speaking, instinctively remaining upwind of the infected man. It is only when the fire begins to smoke and blaze fully that Mossman's last screams suddenly rip from the flames. They all run toward their houses.

He told Charlie what they did—Charlie hollered at him for fifteen minutes, telling him never never never do that again. Dave was shocked at his reaction, insulted, and he went to bed crying and muttering, the hell with you, go to hell, fuck off, I'll do what I want. I know the rules. And a minute later Charlie spoke from the door: "next time leave them alone. Don't try to do anything to them."

"Well *you* do."

"Well, I have to—you don't. No sense in your ending up cooking somewhere in a fire. If you're going to live through this you gotta do what I say. Leave them alone."

And later, lying with his hands behind his head looking out his window at the dying glow from the fires in town, he still felt that funny, rising sensation in his chest, that mixture of calmness and excitement, and no fear.

The flat tasting soup does not satisfy him, and as he rides in the bright, morning light, he shakes slightly, seems not to have full control over his motion. By midmorning hunger gnaws at him, not at his belly but at his physical stability.

He is prepared for this. Riding along on a road indistinguishable from the one running through his town, he looks idly for farms which had gardens next to the houses. Charlie had taught him this trick: gardens are self perpetuating with a kind of retrograde precision. What was once a neatly squared off series of rows of plants becomes a hidden mishmash of food growing itself for no one, obscuring its geometric order in its idle year by year wait for someone to use it. In Hartwick he finds a garden, and inside of five minutes is able to identify a potato plant. He pulls it up, taking five pounds of dirt with it, and suspended in the dirt finds the marble size balls of young potatoes. Next he finds green onions which have spread through the weeds toward the old potato patch. There are ragged vines with small squash blossoms on them. Although there is no fruit on the vines, he knows the flowers themselves are nutritious. He makes a fire and boils the potatoes, onions and blossoms with a pack of soup.

He continues on Route 205 towards Oneonta, burping back the green onions. 205 is a good road, barely affected by the advancing weeds. It runs alongside a hill, so that off to his right, a valley winds its way south. As he rides he takes gulps of boiled water from a plastic thermos mounted on the frame of the bike.

Through Oneonta, a town that apparently survived the first wave since a section of the huge railroad yard was converted into a place for the disposal of the dead. Past the small city and up a long, winding hill, still following Charlie's new directions. It takes him two hours to climb the hill, toward a town called Franklin, and from the top he can see in any direction twenty or thirty kilometers. The sky is a deep, almost dark blue, as if it is space itself he stands in. The hills stretch off with no evidence of humans ever having lived here, green mounds off into infinity.

Harriman—Route 17 is similar in its black dignity to the Thruway. He becomes mesmerized by his own motion, hardly aware of the panorama passing slowly out of his line of vision. When he downshifts on a rise he does it lazily, submitting to his diminished momentum before it is even necessary. He is at peace with his solitude now, almost unafraid of the night, unafraid of the possibility of being watched. The fact of having killed one of the four in Utica braces him.

The mesmerized movement continues as it has since Utica—nothing alters it, not overturned cars, bones, not even the silver hull of a mammoth jet which crashed years ago on a field outside of Harriman. What halts him is a horizontal strip of light, thick in the middle, suggesting something square on the ground. Something huge, perhaps a square kilometer of light, around ten kilometers away. Straddling the bike, he waits for his eyes to adjust to being blinded the moment he broke over the top of a low hill. Squinting, he sees that the square is made up of thousands of tiny dots of orange light. Electricity? He knows by the maps that he is still a long way from the Complex. He makes his precautionary preparations. The bow comes out of the quiver, and straightening it this time he notices that the oil has softened so that there is no resistance in the hinge. He looks around, sees to his left a narrow macadam road snaking up a hill. From the top he might get a better view. Before he turns the bike toward the hill, the lights begin to fade, so that as the front of the grid melts to the back, he squints at it, looking for human activity. Then the entire grid goes out. He waits until the dark orange lights wane into nothing, and removes the sleeping bag from the rear rack, trying to remember if electric lights flash off quickly or fade.

In the morning he sees that the source of lights seems to be objects arranged in a huge square. A quick ride toward them yields the simple information that the source of light was the sun reflecting off the back windows of what seems to him a million new cars boxed in by a cyclone fence twenty feet high, with the same sign every fifteen meters:

Danger!
Electric Fence

> Property of General Motors Corporation—In accordance with Act 0156 persons trespassing will be assumed looters and shot by security guards. Licencee assumes no responsibility for injury.

The cars are all Buick "Viking" Station Wagons, fresh from the Suffern plant, perhaps fifteen years old. It is a model Dave has seen only a few times. He rides along the fence past the almost endless lines of cars, noticing that they are so precisely parked that the corridors of his vision between them fan in forty-five and ninety degree angles off the line of his motion. He knows it is ridiculous to bother, but he decides to ride around the fence. At the back corner he finds that vandals have demolished a section of the fence and have coasted some of the cars through the hole and down a steep embankment into a stream bed. Forty or fifty of them, creating an angular alluvial fan of cars. Inside the fence vandals have broken windows, working in from the hole in the fence—windshields, side windows, mirrors, on about a hundred cars, at which the vandals apparently became exhausted and gave up. One car has a skull impaled on its gear shift lever. Another is decorated with bones inside. In another Dave finds pornographic pictures strewn over the back seat, and he stares at one of a woman and a dog.

He walks toward the center of the lot of cars, realizing that he is tired, and wasting time. He has the vague impulse to get inside one and make believe that he is driving, but he had done this so often as a child that the idea quickly loses its appeal.

On his way back he passes a car and sees three cars away a man sitting with his head in his hands under the upraised door of the station wagon—the bow is out and snapped open with instinctive speed and the arrow is set. Dave stumbles back as the man looks up and glares at him without surprise. "Go ahead," he says, waving at Dave and looking away. "Shoot."

Dave backs away further. The man is probably infected. One pantleg is torn and bloody and he sits with hopeless resignation, with that kind of wan smile that accompanies the blood-shot eyes and the moaning. There is no wind, but in his condition he is dangerous, virile. Dave raises the bow. "Don't you want to play some of your goddamned games?" the man says. "C'mon, where's your buddies?"

"What?" Dave glances down the shimmering corridor towards the hole in the fence. "I don't have any." He backs away further, lowering the bow. "I'm from up north. I'm goin' to the Complex."

The man snorts. "Sure." He looks around, still expecting to see more people. Dave stands with the bow still half drawn, waiting for the man's next move.

"What are you doing up this far? I mean, how far is it to the people?"

"Listen, are you telling the truth? Are you from up north? Nah," he says. "Shoot, get it over with." Then he laughs with limp and hopeless relaxation. "Nobody's alive up there. But I'll tell you, you play a better game than the rest."

"There're a few alive. I'm one of let's see, five, no four, from up by Buffalo. There's some in other towns near us, and supposta be more in Canada. Leastways 'at's what they say."

"What's that accent."

"Huh? Uh, none I know of. *You* sound a little funny to me though. I'm from a place called New Florence, up by Buffalo. Outside forty fifty miles or so."

The man squints at him skeptically, then stands up slowly, favoring the knee. He steps toward Dave, who backs up and draws the bowstring back by way of warning. "Please don't come any closer. My Dad he said if anybody did I should shoot. I don't wanna but—"

"It's okay," the man says. "I'll stay here, right here. Can't walk too well anyway." He stops as if trying to remember something. "Listen, this isn't supposed to be true. They said nobody's alive anywhere but just outside the—"

"Do you have the Ceph?"

"Not that I know of, but with this cut, I'm finished."

"What is the condition of the Complex?"

"It chugs along. Why do you ask?"

"I have a lottery ticket."

"You gotta have a matching number. You know—"

"I have." As the man's expression gradually changes from its look of bland fatigue to a kind of mystified curiosity, Dave's face flushes with anger.

He should not have mentioned the ticket. It means unnecessary vulnerability, a stupid breach of caution.

"Do you know what that means?" the man says. "You'd be the last one in the world. My God it's been years, years." He shakes his head, then waves at Dave as if to change the subject. "Listen, I'd like to talk to you a little bit. First, I'm not after your ticket. Even if I had it I wouldn't use it, because I wouldn't try to go back through that—" and he gestures down the highway, "anyway, listen, let's get out of these cars. I think it might be a little dangerous if we stay. There're miners here, and punks, and—"

"Miners?"

"A nickname for those who go looking for good booze, firearms, metals. Listen, I'll walk over here two cars or so, and we can go parallel out that corner. I'm roasting here."

They walk, Dave keeping his eye on the man's head bobbing irregularly over the tops of the Buicks. He is having trouble with his knee. Dave is still angry at himself for mentioning the ticket, but it's true, the man is probably screwed since he doesn't know how to treat himself, or else he would have. Outside, Dave has to come within five meters of him in order to get around the fence, and he does so quickly, permitting himself one glance to see the man's face clearly. He is younger than he first appeared. He gets his distance again and returns to his shooting stance, the bow partly drawn, the arrow pointing down at the ground.

"Christ you're cautious," the man says. "I mean Jesus, this is crazy."

"It's how I stay alive. My Dad tol' me—"

"Yeah, yeah," the man says, laughing. "Jesus." Trying to act nonchalant, he moves further away from Dave toward a tree, next to which stands the bicycle.

"Wait," Dave says. The man stops. "Stand clear over by the fence." When he does so, hobbling, Dave retrieves his bicycle and walks it back to his spot by the fence. "Okay, sit there if you want."

"Sure thing chief," the man says, hobbling back.

"Where are you going?" Dave asks.

"I don't know for sure, but I thought I'd go see if it was possible to live away from the rest. Me and my girl were on our way up, you know, when the punks—" He stops and looks back down the highway. "The kids down there—they— Well, I'll skip the details. They killed her. Only advice I have is to run from them. They don't care about getting close to people. Listen, what's up north?"

"What there always was I 'magine. Best thing to do is find old gardens and stuff. Some food left here and there too. Can always grow it too. That you gotta do eventually. Towns've all been looted, 'cause lots of them lasted through the first two waves."

"Aha, yeah, because it's rural I bet. And colder. Around here almost everything went in the first. Then there was the migration." Dave squints. "Yeah, after the first wave there were traffic jams all over, people coming to the Complex, ones with tickets, ones without. Years ago, when they first came out with those medications. Then there was that smelly dust on everything—the antibacterial stuff."

"What's it like now? I mean around the Complex?"

The man makes a brief description: concentric circles, the worst on the outside. In the inner ring, next to the Complex, they get some electrical power and the inner and middle rings get food by military delivery from the Complex, mostly in the form of fish cakes and strange medicated breads made out of plankton. Then there is the Ceph. Summer is bad. This is why the man and his girl left, because the weather is bad again this year. Periodic outbreaks are controlled by barbaric means, at least as far as the afflicted are concerned—if the Complex gets wind of anything like an outbreak, it sends out helicopters and field military personnel to identify the break. If it is real, the militarys evacuate and the copters spray lethal gasses on the infected areas. "Sectors, they call it," he says. The clean stay in their houses, ride out the gas. The infected are driven by their madness into the streets. The spraying goes on for a week, then clean up militarys come in.

The conversation turns from Dave's curiosity about life around the Complex to the man's curiosity about the lack of it upstate. Yes, you can live comfortably if you know how. Water is no problem. Look for gardens, learn how to identify seeds for growing your own food. Boil everything. You'll be okay if you're careful. Read the *Time* Survival Handbook.

"I can't read," he says. "Only numbers, a few words."

"Well, there ain't much to do up there—crack a small town library and live there. You can learn to read. Just use kids' books. Then find the *Boy Scout Handbook*, a couple general medical books, and pamphlets and stuff about growing food."

"*Boy Scout Handbook*? Why that?"

"Got all sorts of stuff about everything. Pictures, too."

"Did you read all that stuff?"

"My Dad made me memorize most of it."

"And what about this?" He points to his knee.

"There's only one good way I know of," Dave says. "When did it happen?"

"Yesterday."

"How bad?" He pulls his pantleg up. The wound is a dirty abrasion, still bleeding out from under the brown scab. "Okay, my Dad had this way, only way it works. Medicines no good for anything—he said that you gotta avoid systemic medicine cause it screws up defenses you have naturally. I'll show you."

It is a strange sensation. He goes about Charlie's method with calm and almost businesslike quickness, suddenly enjoying the company of the man. He is not sure why, but being with somebody is fun. He builds the fire, finds the flat piece of metal and sterilizes it. "Okay, bend your leg tight and tear off the scab and make it bleed like hell." The man sits a minute and considers, finally shrugs. He follow's Dave's directions, his breath jerking as he slowly pulls off the scab, making little sounds in his throat like someone slowly being dipped into cold water. Dave moves to within twenty feet of the man and says, "take this knife and make some cuts around the edges and in the middle, not too deep."

"What? Come on—"

"Do it—it's the only way. You gotta clean it." And so the man does it, again making the sounds in his throat, wincing at his knee. He gestures to throw the knife back.

"No, keep it," Dave says. Next, he flips the hot piece of metal toward the man using two little sticks to launch it. The man pulls it toward himself with a series of quick snatches. "Okay, let the blood drip on the middle of the thing." He does so, and the metal is cool enough now so the blood does not fry on contact. Dave walks to his bike bag. "Okay, bring the blood over to the fire and dry it on that thing." The man does so, looking at him with a grimace of pain and suspicion. The blood slowly turns a deep brick red color as it dries. Dave gets out the cleanest piece of cloth he can find, a once worn pair of underpants. "Okay, now take the—No, here, here's a spoon." He throws it into the fire. "Let it sit a few seconds, then pulverize the blood into a powder." The man follows the instructions, frequently glancing up at Dave with suspicion. "Okay, put the powder right on the cut—pack it on until the wet blood makes a mush of the powder, then tie this rag on."

It dawns on the man. "Instant scab," he says.

"Right—it's a lot better than medicine. It's sterile, too."

"Jesus. Who figured this out? Did you figure this out?"

"My Dad found it in some old papers—it's something they did hundreds of years ago."

Dave's fingers are sore from holding the bow at quarter cock, so he lets it back. They talk. He finds himself describing waves, fires, families going down in volleys of flying bullets. Finally he says, "One time, maybe six years ago," and he sees it again now, briefly, just a flash across the field of his vision, a fast swoop, soundless and graceful, so fast that identification is barely possible in that last gentle trajectory, "I saw a bird."

"A bird?" the man says, his attention drawn from his knee, "you saw a bird?"

"Up near where I live."

"No, that's not possible. All the reports from the reconnaissance say that there isn't anything anywhere. If it's warm blooded it's dead."

"They're wrong. 'sides, I'm warm blooded an' I don't feel dead. You don't look it either."

The man laughs, then looks away as if he is distracted. "Could be," he says. "They might not want to tell—that could be true." He gestures at the highway. "If there was anything alive they wouldn't tell us. That might be."

"I don't understand."

"This argument's been going on for years. The only source of information is the Complex. Some say the best way to get rid of the Ceph is to get rid of those who have it, or could get it."

"But there are millions of—"

"Yeah yeah, I know. It's just that all the people outside are suspicious. Y'know, high death rate, all that."

"But getting rid of all the people doesn't mean getting rid of the Ceph."

"It might—suppose there was the Complex, and no other population. In twenty years or so, no bug, see?"

"Well, I'm goin' in."

The man thinks again. "You saw a bird."

"Yup, after the second wave, long after. Listen, are there a lot of people leaving the Complex, or the rings around it?"

"Yeah, some younger types. Get tired of hanging around to die. They never come back. Probably dead."

"How old are you."

"Huh? Oh, not sure, but twenty-five if what they told me is right."

"I heard that the life span is twenty-four or something."

"Not much more. Listen, you'll hit the bad stuff down about thirty kilometers, around past the Jersey state line. The regular people are south of that. Campers and punks around Ramsey, Ridgewood. Remember those names. And you can see the Complex from Waldwick. Leave the highway and go up any of those steep streets, and look south."

"What about getting into the inner ring?"

"No way I can think of except shooting your way in. You good with that thing?"

"Yup," Dave says. "I killed a guy in Utica, hundred-fifty, two-hundred kilometers up. There were four of them."

"Those are miners," the man said. "They go for booze, firearms, metals, gold and stuff, and sell it to the Complex authorities, or sell it in the inner ring."

"What do they buy?"

"You name it—food, more booze, girls, and then there's the point system for getting into the Complex. If a guy manages to mine enough metals, say, he gets enough points to get in. I didn't know anybody who ever made it, but they say if a guy can bring in enough, he can qualify for entry, either into the Complex as a military or as field militarys, who have their own mini-complexes. Can't go in the big one cause they patrol the perimeter." He looks down the highway, then north. "Hey listen, if I'm gonna find food—"

"Wait." Dave walks to his bike and opens the little bag mounted on the frame. He takes out three little potatoes and one of two remaining bags of soup. "Here." He approaches to within twenty feet, and throws the potatoes and soup to him. "The soup's good, kinda flat, and the potatoes come from one of the gardens I tol' you about. Be sure to boil it. Next town you get to, go to the stores and get pots and stuff. You can cut the soup with clover and stuff for roughage. Just don't use any weeds with milky sap."

"Milky sap. Okay." He looks into his hand. "These are potatoes? Funny, I always thought they would be green."

"And here," Dave says, digging into his pocket, "here's a pack of matches—you gotta have matches."

"Thanks. Hey, what are my chances, with the knee I mean?"

"Fifty-fifty?"

"Well," he says. "that's good enough for me. Okay," he says, looking north again. "Oh, listen, don't tell anybody about the ticket. They'll kill you for it. You gotta take it to the authorities."

"You got a weapon?"

"Yeah, back there—a slingshot with these steel balls they used to use in some Japanese pinball game. Really heavy. I wouldn't like to be hit by one."

"Sounds good," Dave says, "but you gotta practice until you can hit somebody in the head. And if anybody gets any closer than me, shoot."

"Yeah, and what was that, the Boy Scout Handbook?"

"Yeah—you'll find it in the library." The man looks north again, mouthing the words, slowly rubbing his injured knee.

"Anything else I should know?"

"About a thousand things, but a lot comes down to trying to eat the same kinds of things, stay away from what you don't know about. Keep your teeth clean—cavities and abcesses, you're finished. You gotta keep your teeth clean. When you wash, don't use soap. Your skin's gotta have its oil all the time. Don't get sunburns—"

"Okay okay," he says, laughing, "that's all I can handle."

"And learn to read," Dave says. "You gotta learn to read."

Route Seventeen again. Dave is exhausted, dazed from talking to the man. Talking, with the necessity to remain on guard every second, is physical effort more demanding than pumping up a five kilometer hill. Ramsey, Allendale, Waldwick. Bergen Avenue is one of a number of streets going up to his right. He must walk the bike up past the small houses. The hill is very steep. Vandals have coasted cars down so that some of the houses have their rear ends protruding out of livingrooms into the high weeds. On top, Dave looks south and sees nothing—or perhaps sees something but does not know how to identify what he sees. The sky looks grey rather than blue, and he can see buildings, probably in the outlying cities of New Jersey across the river from the Complex. He stands there a full thirty seconds, his eyes searching into the washed out grey, and it materializes slowly, in strange shifts of the eye, as if the view of it was hidden from him only because of its immensity. It was there all along.

A shape. Yes, there it is—the eye jerks around it in order to give it definition. There it is. Blakely's Ark. It is a honeycombed mountain—he squints. He sees the chambered extensions, the sections crawling out over the river and into the marshlands of eastern New Jersey. The closer sections are clearer. They may be only fifty kilometers away. The gates of the new world only a half a day's slow ride. He will present his ticket to a uniformed man, who will assign him a residence unit. Where? In which of the multitude of mammoth sections? My God, he thinks. A fortress. A miniature universe. Enough space for twenty million people to live. And no Ceph. No fires, corpses, decomposition, a smell as familiar to him as sweat. All of those things that Charlie warned were possibly fatal: bumping into someone, drinking a glass of water, taking a bath, eating strange food, would now become mindlessly common acts.

When Dave was a boy Charlie showed him an old science book. In one picture, sitting precariously on the edge of the Grand Canyon an artist had superimposed a photograph of a box, and in it, the caption said, the entire population of the world would fit, like sardines stacked shoulder to foot. Dave used to imagine, sometimes even have bad dreams about what would happen if the box fell into the canyon. It would split, and waves of human flesh would run into the Colorado River. Fissures would emit flesh. Little avalanches would make a dam. He sees the shape before him as the box on the canyon come true. The man who designed the Complex died before it was started, not of Ceph but of suicide. Charlie said it was three times the size of Blakely's original plan, double the size of the Black Sea Dome and seven times larger than the eight or nine successful small complexes all over the globe.

Charlie's book: 'from any point inside the Jersey line leave route Seventeen. Celetti says that the vandals have that road controlled. He says that you should go west about a mile and find a parallel route called Franklin Turnpike, an old road which runs next to what used to be the Erie Railroad and is now a mass transit track. In any case, follow Franklin Turnpike as far as you can, and around Hawthorne it will lead to a gate into the middle ring.' The principle is that Dave should travel through close groupings of houses so as not to be noticed at a distance. Franklin Turnpike, shaded by huge maples, is a small four lane street with old houses just on the other sides of its sidewalks. Almost like a tunnel, it goes straight toward the Complex. There is much more debris on it than on the highway, and Dave notices too that there is no longer any open space, no chance to find gardens or wild food in the woods. This is the trouble spot, the last bottle-neck. He rides the Turnpike at middle speed, constantly darting wary glances around him. Paterson is only fifteen kilometers away. Just beyond that he will be safe.

He is thinking, *a half hour's ride, that's all, just*—and sees a biker flash across a distant intersection at blistering speed. There is something strange about the way he is dressed. Dave stops. Straddling his seat, he takes his bow off from its position binding on his chest, and removes a hunting arrow from the quiver. He holds both in his hand as he coasts slowly toward the intersection. If he moves fast—

Now behind him: someone makes a weird noise.

"Nguack?" A chicken? "Nguack? Ak ak, nguack?" No, he is imitating a duck. That's it—ducks quacked. Dave sees him now, a skinny boy riding along without touching his handgrips, coming toward him from seventy-five meters away.

Dave pulls the bike off the street and roots the arrow, and his mouth fills with the taste of dry copper. A strange little group congregates two blocks down the Turnpike. They laugh and talk, all straddling their bikes. Dave glances quickly at the darkened windows of the houses, and then back to the group. One of them is a girl, and at first he cannot be sure—yes, she is wearing some kind of a tight fitting suit with the top cut out so that her breasts protrude into the air. The fast biker pulls up next to them. He wears some kind of an old fashioned costume, tight fitting gold pants with a jacket, ruffles under his chin and a shiny wig on his head. He wears a whip coiled up on his belt.

Some of the people are not full grown. The duck guy behind him has stopped and is keeping his distance. "Nguack?"

"Where's Big John?" the whip man asks.

"Here." He is closer than any of them. One block away, dressed in blue jeans and a leather jacket and cowboy hat. He has a stringy beard and long hair. Saluting formally, he says, "Lookee lookee lookee, a brand new cookie."

Dave holds the arrow in position and looks from one point to the other, his heart thumping loudly in his ears and his knees like rubber. The smell of his fear rises around his face. He feels sweat trickling in his hair. Big John stands just out of range and nods at him, then yells to the little group, "Aw come on up and say hello! Where are your manners?"

The girl approaches, walking with an exaggerated sway in her hips. Dave gets off the bike and lets it fall into the weeds. The whip man approaches behind the girl, takes the whip off his belt and snaps it lightly at her feet. She turns, says something to him. Duck waits. Big John signals to the girl.

"Where are you going?" she calls with bright curiosity.

"Listen, I'm good with this. Don't come any closer."

"Are you all right? Not sick?" she says. "Nobody wants to hurt you honey." She is only fifteen meters away. "Can I come closer, just to look at you?" She continues, stepping cautiously toward him, her hands under her breasts. Dave half raises the bow. "You wouldn't do that would you?" she says. "Listen, we aren't like the others." Her voice is soft and soothing, almost a breathless whine. "Big John sent me to tell you that we're nice. He told me that to make your travels happy that I should split my chops for you." Everyone laughs. Big John slaps his knees.

"Back up," Dave says.

"Son," Big John says, "we'll show you what she means."

This excites them all. "Nguack? Nguackackack?"

The whip man draws back and snaps. The littler boys approach in whispers. "We will treat you to an exhibition."

"I don't want no exhibition."

"You sound like—like a foreigner," she says, her voice high and soft, "are you a foreigner?"

"I'm from upstate. You stay back now."

"Don't you want to dip it in my soup?" she asks. "Churn my butter? I'm *yummy*." She is too close. Ten meters. She unzips part of the tight fitting suit so her belly shows. "Now don't use that thing," she says, "just watch."

Duck and Big John seem content to stand where they are and watch. The smaller boys fade into closer camouflage. Whip is twenty meters behind the girl who is pulling off the suit, until all that is left are her frayed pink pants. She begins to dance, holding her arms out with her eyes sad, her hands hanging limply at the ends of her arms. She sings softly, "—beautiful for spacious skies, for amber waves of hmmmm, purple mountains," and grabs the breasts, "—fruity plain." Dave listens for telltale sounds near him—escape between the houses won't work because of the bike in the high weeds.

"Whatcha got in the bike bag tough guy?" Big John asks.

"Let me go by. Just let me go by."

"Jesus, you missed the fuckin' Hudson Gate by a long shot—you got a turd in your brain?"

"What's he wearin' those funny clothes for?" Dave asks.

"Oh, the asshole saw a movie once—hasn't been the same since. I think he looks like a fag."

"Hey," Whip says to Big John, "how about sitting on this?" He holds his whip handle up.

"You're not looking at me," the girl says, stopping. "He doesn't even want to *look*. What do I have to do?"

"He's a picky shithead isn't he? Show him the rest."

She pulls off the pink pants. Dave's eyes fix for a moment on the black triangle between her legs.

"Now I ask you," John says, "is there a finer grade "A" prime U. S. Government 'spected piece of meat than that? Look, we like you. We'd like you to join our little group here. We make raids into shitsville. We sack miners. We live a high old life." He waits a moment for Dave to speak, then begins to shake his head. "You're nasty," he says. "You're like all the other goddam miners we meet. Know what we do? We hang them from their own guts." The girl collects her clothes, holds her middle finger out to Dave and walks away.

"So we're gonna hang you from your *own guts*!"

John says, his voice rising into a loud and intense whisper. "You've insulted *my gash*. I could almost cry I'm so disappointed."

From thirty meters away the girl yells out, "boo–hoo, oh boo–hoo! I'm so em*bar*rassed, I feel rotten!"

They have all faded back. Dave's heart thumps faster and he quickly shakes the sweat from his face. This strategy precedes attack. "I'm just dis*gus*ted with you. You've ruined my day completely." It is almost as if the response precedes the sound: Dave has pulled off at a form to his left and sees the little boy five meters away fall into the weeds, the arrow having slapped his middle open and a long object, a blowgun, trailing out of his right hand behind him. Dave roots another arrow and stands. He must concentrate to figure out if he has been hit.

Duck raises a short rifle to his cheek. No, a crossbow. Dave grabs the bike and runs into the weeds next to the house. The crossbow arrow thwocks into the corner Dave hides behind. "You can't get away from us miner," John says. "It's useless—we're gonna gut you."

Then, "Nguack? Nguack?"

They have him cornered, but seem in no rush to get him. He draws the arrow back, hooks his index finger gently into the corner of his mouth and presents himself at the corner of the house. Stones hit the wall above him. Duck, still straddling his bike, aims. Dave lets off and returns to his hiding place. He hears a scream and then a loud choking sound, and peeks. Duck is running around making believe the arrow hit him in the crotch. "My manhood!" he screams, "right in the cock!" John laughs. Dave roots another arrow and repeats his quick shot. This time it is close enough to drive Duck away. When he returns to his spot Dave sees that another boy has made it into the back yard and he draws the bow and aims just as the boy rises from the weeds to throw a rock. He sees Dave and immediately drops the rock and in a sniveling, sob-choked voice says, "please don't—I didn't mean anything."

"Get out of here," Dave says, and the kid runs.

Duck is no longer blocking his way back toward Bergen Avenue. Dave must go now. He positions the bow on his chest with the string binding, grabs his bike and runs so that the quiver bangs against his back. He mounts and wheels off. "Hey, *get* 'im," John yells, and Duck yells back, "Bastard nicked my leg!" Bergen Avenue—he skims around the corner and down the hill toward the highway at a dangerous speed, the wind driving the sweat from his forehead into his eyes. On the highway he aims for the Complex, but before he has gone three hundred meters sees that he is being followed. The three bigger boys skim along behind him at more than his speed, and he shifts into high and pumps with steady, hard strokes, his body down and the wind pressing at his eyes. He is moving so fast that the heavy quiver is lifted by the wind from his back. He must veer off again toward the turnpike because coming in his direction are two bikes, ridden by boys naked to the waist and painted in bright colors. One has a huge eye on his chest, the other a blue skull. They are muscular and their heads are shaved except for strips of short hair over the top from the front to the back. Mohicans they used to be called. They are not interested in him. Half a block into a side road Dave stops, his legs trembling with fatigue and the metally saliva thick in his mouth. The two painted boys have stopped and are facing the group of Dave's pursuers who have stopped. The boy with the skull on his chest reaches into a bike bag and pulls out a pistol. "We got a gun," he yells.

"Prove it shithead," John yells.

He raises it, aims, and there is a hollow crack and a puff of smoke.

"Where'd you get it?"

"We borrowed it from a miner." Everyone laughs.

"Wanna make a raid?"

"Okay. We got the gun we got first choice on the chow. Fifty fifty on the pussy." More laughter. "Deal? Hey, you Big John? I'm Snake Patzert." John waves.

"Hey Snake," he says. "You're the one who likes to cut heads off? I heard of you—you're kinda famous around here for rolling heads."

"Well, it's just a thing I got. Screwed up childhood y' know." They laugh. Whip and John talk. By this time they have been joined by the girl and a couple of the smaller boys.

"Deal," John says. "Trade you first choice on the chow for a hump apiece on this one."

The two painted boys talk. Then, "Hey sweets? Come a little closer." She walks down the highway toward them. They watch her for ten seconds, talking. "Okay, okay, deal, but we want sweetie first. Later we'll boogie—rolling heads and bonfires and booze and all. Throw in with us and we got a goddam head rollin' army—we'll set a head rollin' record."

"Okay, but there's a miner up there somewhere. I wanna gut the son of a bitch. Slipped by this dummy here. He was licking a scratch on his stupid goddam leg."

"Nosireebobby," the eye says, "the slit comes first."

"He killed one of my boys."

"Aww gee—" and they laugh. "Boo-hoo." John watches silently. "Tough tittie. I'm so *hurt* for you!"

"Okay, okay." The two groups cautiously approach each other.

* * *

Night. He sits in a straightbacked chair to keep himself partially awake, and looks at the front door, waiting. On the couch is a webbed skeleton. His bow sits at his side next to two hunting arrows, his bike stands at his other side. He breathes evenly, frequently feeling his breath halt on the intake, jerking with silent sobs. He is only a quarter of a mile from the spot where he first saw the awesome form of the Complex materialize before him. Little sounds, wind against windows, flies, unidentifiable sounds from outside, make him jump, tense up and stare with his breath held. The hot, yawning vacuum of his hunger surges in slow waves, making his heart beat and his forehead bead with sweat. The need to sleep gradually overcomes his fear and hunger.

He jerks up to the light. It is morning. Out through the translucent curtains he sees smoke billowing into the sky to the south. He sits up, feeling his stomach contract in pain. In the wind he smells the familiar odors of decay and charred wood. He listens for a long time for the sounds of punks, but hears nothing.

Out to the road then for another crack at Hawthorne. Again he approaches the crossroads where he first saw the frilled biker, but this time there is no one. Past that corner by two hundred yards he skims by and does not look long at a corpse staked out hand and foot on a rubblestrewn front yard, apparently murdered by the punks. He rides now with the bow in his right hand, and negotiates the bike past the cars and the litter with his left. Whole blocks of houses have been burned, and he feels a frightening insecurity at riding by in plain sight.

Five blocks into a town called Hohokus he sees off to his left a group of punks sitting around a fire eating. They see him but are not interested. Ridgewood: the panorama changes. At the bottom of every hill the streets are choked with cars. There are skulls impaled on the steel steps on the telephone poles, nooses are hung from trees with piles of bones underneath. On the near horizon he sees more smoke from small fires.

During his hourlong journey to the border of the middle ring he continually expects to be seen by punks. Their fires hover within a hundred meters of his passing, the evidence of their recent activity assaults his sense of smell. At one point he even hears them yelling about something and is almost caught except for their interest in chasing one of their own, a kid who protests that he has a cold, only a cold, but they laugh and disregard his explanation and giddily prepare their weapons on the run and build a fire. The poor kid manages to throw only one rock before being lassoed, and is barely into a squeaking argument against their convictions when the boss punk sneaks up behind him and shoots him in the back of the head.

While they drag the body toward the fire, Dave slips past. He continues on his way into Hawthorne toward Paterson. The obstruction of his vision by buildings decreases gradually—they are reduced here to blackened foundations, the road is glutted with rubble. The border is a devastated no man's land garbage dump—he straddles the bike and looks across the border at a makeshift fence, behind which he can see the lowhanging smoke from a million fires, which obscures the Complex. All he needs to do is make it the last two hundred meters and go through what looks like billows of barbed wire fence and old doors. Beyond that the buildings look whole, with windows. The streets will be clean, there will be people—*ticket should give you legal right to pass*. Only two hundred meters to the beginning of civilization.

He walks the bike forty meters, sees a puff of smoke, hears something bong an old car behind him and hears the shot. He trots the bike back to safety. He must work his way along and look for a gate of some kind.

He makes two more tries this day. Each appearance into the no man's land brings about the appearance of men behind the barbed wire, their weapons out. He is not even close enough to talk. He is growing exhausted with his hunger and lack of sleep, and begins to involuntarily curl himself around the foul and acidic vacuum below his ribs. Worse is the trembling and the unexpected waves of sweat, symptoms which seem suspiciously similar to those of the Ceph.

Near sundown, after passing by areas where he can clearly see the clean looking houses and the people, he encounters more punks on the border. Again they are dressed in strange costume. The boys, about four or five of them, wear tight fitting leather, the two girls wear shining fur coats. They sit silently around a fire, each separated from the other by a body's length distance. Assuming that this caution indicates sanity, he prepares to yell to them, but before he is able to he sees that one younger boy has risen from the fire, and in a familiar exasperation has gone behind a low foundation to vomit. He hears the retching, sees the wan and disinterested response of the others, who hunch in their fur and leather. Ceph. He must make a wide circle around them. That familiar, coppery taste fills his mouth. Oh yes, you must never let up your guard. Never. The germ is everywhere, under every board, hitching rides on every insect, in fact could now be riding dormant in the currents of your saliva. Anything you touch could be tainted, any person you see can carry in him the capacity to kill you at twenty feet just because of an unexpected gust of wind. It is no wonder they shoot at him from across the border.

Dave is shocked at seeing the vomiting boy—he holds in his dying body the superior being of the universe, the nullifier of everything, the agent which makes all beings not huddling behind twenty feet of reinforced concrete in a deadened atmosphere, all beings, stumblingly hopeless wretches just a hair's breadth this side of being maggot food. He is suddenly so awed by the power of it that he wants to go to the little group and wallow, infect himself, give in to it. He has that strange conviction that avoiding the disease is not possible, and if it is possible then it is not worth the trouble. In the advancing twilight he looks across the border at the buildings. Above them, in the mist, he sees small points of light, kilometers away, and realizes that they are too high in the sky to be from any other source but the Complex.

II

Almost twenty-four hours later, his head hot and his knees threatening to buckle, he walks the bike around the corner of a foundation and sees less than a kilometer away, down dark green bluffs, the Hudson River. It disappears into a mammoth cement mouth, which looks like a broad frown. It is the apron on the northern edge of the grey mountain of Complex, according to the book, the Hudson Gate. He had stumbled along, frequently doubling back, searching along devastated streets in Fair Lawn, Glen Rock, Oradell, Dumont. He had climbed banks, the bike on his shoulder, onto new highways littered with rubble. Each attempt at the border was repulsed. And now, having just crossed 9-W, he has made it to the Palisades Interstate, the miner's approach to the

Complex. He squints down at it, sees forms, people milling about. They are probably passing their goods to the outer extensions of the Complex, trading for their points, all below the monstrous domes with their portholes, where helicopters hover like bees around the entrance to a hive. From here the Complex looks something like a rounded pyramid constructed of a million tubular domes.

Outside it there are twenty- and thirty-story buildings, some occupied judging from the smoke from small fires around them. Helicopters sweep along the apron, and he can hear the flopflop-flopflapflapflatflat propeller sound changing in tone as they tip in graceful circles low over the marshy no-man's land between the Complex and the buildings closest to it in the inner ring. The population is sparse here—the rings thin out, because the northern side of the Complex is its remotest corner.

Slowly negotiating the bike down a winding road through the Hudson River bluffs he repeats in his mind, almost as if it is a prayer, no it is not Ceph, it is only hunger. Hunger makes you feel sick. Makes you dizzy. Makes you want to puke. The acidic gnawing is aggravated by the little jounces and bumps of the ride. The uniformed men he approaches argue with a man who gestures at a small trailer hitched to a bicycle.

"You guys don't know what we go through up there—"

"Fifteen."

"I about busted my ass getting this here. It's pure copper, man. Thirty's more like it."

"If you don't like the rates then try selling it in Chicago."

"Har har har. Joker. Okay, gimme the goddamned points."

Dave's turn. He approaches to within twenty feet. "I got a ticket."

"Just cut the horseshit and state what you've got."

"It's the truth. I got a ticket and you're supposta let me through. You're police aren't you?" They snort and grin at each other. One elbows his shoulderslung automatic weapon behind him and steps closer.

"Come on over here then." Dave straddles the bike, watches the miner recede into the distance, pulling his copper toward the Complex. True, he can't show anybody anything unless he is prepared to approach. He will not throw the ticket to the man. He must let him handle it. Just as he is about to hold it out, he sees in a ditch beyond the men a corpse covered with white powder.

"What happened to him?"

"He stepped on a nail."

"Why the hell doesn't anybody ever say the truth?"

"Listen boy, you either state what you carry and hand it over for your goddam points or you get the hell outta here. Alright alright, that guy came crawling in here this morning, so we drilled him. Summertime is game time for the germ, and you act a little funny yourself." The second guard snorts.

"Okay okay," Dave says, approaching cautiously. His mind ticks off the breaches of caution as he closes in: safe, unsafe on windy day, very dangerous, certain death. He holds the lottery ticket out, his head involuntarily turning away from the man he stands too close to. He barely breathes, cannot avoid looking at the little moles, pits, lines, peculiarities of the man's face. The only other human he has been this close to is Charlie.

"Relax," the guard says. He takes the ticket, wearing plastic gloves. "Big deal. I got one too. Let's see the papers."

"Give me back the ticket first." He hands it back. His hand shaking, Dave holds it by a corner and wonders what to do with it.

"C'mon," the guard says, "you're not gonna catch it just—"

"Well I can!" His voice quakes in childish falsetto.

The guard looks at his papers, again elbowing the automatic behind him. "Well. What the hell took you so long? You mean you been living in, uh, New Florence, New York all these years? How?"

"Lemme see that," the other guard says. "Is it—"

"Yowzah—perfect match. Hey kid, you're headlines."

"Perfect match shit," the second guard says. "How long'd it take you to make this, fucker?"

"It's *real*," Dave says. " 'sides, it's not for you to figure that out. Just let me through so I can—"

"Let you through," the second guard snarls, "I oughtta cut you in half right now. I figure you're a punk who—"

"Stewart," the first guard says, "easy, he's right. It isn't for you to figure out."

"I need food."

"Don't we all," Stewart says.

"Relax kid. Wait." The first guard goes into a low cement building and comes back out with something wrapped in dull foil. Dave rips the foil open with trembling hands in a kind of exasperated urgency, and eats. It is salty, strong flavored. "What's this?"

"Ground up Ceph victims, a little maggot puree—"

Dave is spitting it out, gagging, almost vomiting when the first guard laughs heartily and says, "Wait, I'm only kidding. Wait wait wait wait. Listen, it's protein, fish and beans and stuff. It's medicated." He nods reassuringly, still laughing, and Dave goes on eating slowly.

"Hey kid," Stewart says, "you don't look so good."

"Stewart," the first guard says, "relax. Let him alone."

Dave stops in mid-chew, stares at Stewart, who smiles back.

"I'm hungry is all. I don't have the bug."

"But look at his eyes. Bloodshot? He shakes too."

"Stewart, the book says clearly distinguishable symptoms. Wait for somebody else to shoot, huh?"

Dave washes down the salty breadlike material with water from his bike thermos, looks once at the dust covered corpse, and coughs a little water into the back of his nose.

"Okay kid," the first guard says, "answer the following questions: one, did you encounter any persons on your way in?"

He coughs, clears his throat. "Utica. Four guys who took my food, shot at me. I killed one."

"You assholes. There's so much stuff to mine up there—"

"It wasn't my *fault*," Dave whines. "Some people in a place called Waldwick. Killed one there."

"Punks. Shoulda killed them all."

"And about, oh, fifteen kilometers back along the edge there I saw about eight or nine, different ages, all with the bug. Puking, sitting around hunched up." The guard stops, looks up.

"Eight? On the perimeter? When?"

"Yesterday."

"How close did you approach?"

"Long distance. Fifty sixty meters. No wind either. Went way way way around them. Way way around. Real far—"

"Okay okay, you convinced me. Stewart, call."

Stewart goes into the low cement building. Through the doorway Dave sees him talking into what looks like a walkie talkie. It takes about thirty seconds. From above the cement mouth into which flows the Hudson River rise two helicopters, which immediately tip and soar over their heads with the deafening clackclackflackflackflockflopfloptuptup-tup—

"Do they spray them?" Dave shouts.

"Spray the whole area."

"Why don't they go spray the punks?"

"Range. Anybody inside a certain distance might as well shoot himself sooner or later. Up outside forty kilos or so, the copters don't go because it's too far—too much fuel. That's why they hang around so far outside the perimeter."

"Where do I go from here?"

"Straight down the highway. It runs along the wire. Don't touch anything on the apron. It's mined, it has trip wires and gas jets all over the place. You have to go into what they call the West New York Gate. In New Jersey, down the fence about six kilometers. Now first go into the—"

—outer population by old mainstreet routes he went, passing small buildings, large houses, all with fires going, with children playing on lawns, with older people in shirt-sleeves and naked to the waist working outside on various means of upkeep of their places, mending watertanks and solar converters on housetops, tilling small gardens, standing in groups laughing and talking, each time suddenly becoming silent as he passed on his bike. He saw too, for the first time in his life, Negroes, with skin the color of polished floors or stair bannisters, standing out on the streets in little groups. As he proceeded through the middle ring the panorama became more dense, the buildings larger, closer set, the streams of people moving on the streets heavier. Again, as he had encountered in first approaching the middle ring yesterday, he found that his road progressing toward the West New York Gate was blocked, and there was another rubblestrewn and wireclogged no-man's land. No soldiers patrolled it. Beyond that, up in the smoky atmosphere, he was presented with another profile of the cement mountain. From here it appeared to be long, something like on of the old cruise ships with stacks of levels going to the top. From the books about it he knew it stretched from the Hudson Gate fringe in Yonkers all the way to the tip of old Manhattan, across both rivers into the mainland and into Brooklyn to the east. Blakely's plan was to appropriate the Hudson as a food and fresh water source, use the bay as an outlet for fishing expeditions, and build the principle structure on the island of Manhattan, which was, he said somewhere, the strongest natural foundation of any of the possible sites considered at the outset of the plan. They tried building them in a number of large cities, but catastrophic outbreaks, panic, and finally a choice of one site, made in desperation by legislators in Washington, left them with this one.

He saw no way of going through the fence and into the inner ring without becoming a target on his way. Dusk approached, and he knew that he had to find a place to sleep before trying the border tomorrow.

He had always preferred sleeping in his bag in some rudimentary shelter because there was never anything tangible to fear. Enclosures were always dangerous, and so he got used to avoiding them. Now, in the ring of population surrounding the Complex, he needed a place with a door he could lock, and it became apparent in a half hour that he would not find one:

"But it's empty up there. Can't I just pass the apartments and go up the stairs?"

"Set foot in here and you'll regret it, chief."

"But up on the fourth floor. All above is empty, right?"

"Move on buddy. Just move on."

New streets tantalized him with the suggestion of

open space on the other end, and each time he arrived at new groupings of buildings and new concentrations of people. Anything that could have been an enclosure had already been reduced to neat stacks of firewood. Property was owned by the occupiers and the use of back lawns, garages, alleys between houses was forbidden, always with the suggestion that if he set foot in these areas it meant instant physical retaliation.

He slept in an alley between two tall buildings, behind a pile of garbage that no one claimed as property. It was the worst night of all. Throughout, the dull orange glow of fires illuminated the dirty bricks across the alley above the garbage pile, which seemed to consist mostly of wet and stinking rags and buckets with bottoms rotted out. Although this was the most anonymous place he could find, it was too vulnerable to permit him to sleep. Shadows of roaming boys flashed across the high wall his eyes groggily rested on. The shouts of kids raising hell came from all directions. At one point a man wandered into his alley to urinate unsteadily, mumbling to himself and aiming at some can in the pile, so that the heavy drumming sound made the content of his mumbling unintelligible. Over a wooden wall at the back of the alley a group of boys apparently took turns on a girl who forced them to give her 'scrip' before she let them. Dave sat with his bow strung and hunting arrow out, listening to the giggles and goodhumored protests of the girl (you dirty pig Georgie—why do you want to do *that*?). The other boys argued over who was next. Somewhere out on the street men seeking vengeance caught their prey and beat him until they were tired, and for the next hour Dave heard the victim's garbled and thickly nasal moans.

Toward dawn there came the distant sounds of violence, screams, shouts of protest, wailing sobs. Just before the light began to come, he dozed for a time with the sounds continuing, and then awoke and sat wide-eyed staring at the bricks, thinking, this is it, this is the core of filth of the whole world. He couldn't believe it—nobody had a chance in a place like this. The place crawled with punks, but here their existence was kept secret only by the greater number of their victims. Nobody seemed to care about the bug—the need to satisfy the lust for brutality and mutilation seemed more important. Rising to walk out into the harsh light of morning, he thought, I gotta get outta here.

Food. He had no idea what he was supposed to do to get it, but knew from the book that it was distributed at various points throughout the populated areas. He wandered through the streets, walking his bicycle, observing the morning chores of the people. Doors opened and arcs of yellow liquid shot out, catching the sunlight briefly before splattering into the gutter. People walked around carrying large buckets or wheeling them on makeshift wagons. In one spot, near a group of closely packed old buildings, he saw that they were taking the buckets to water tanks towed in by small square vehicles of the type he had seen in pictures of old airports. He needed no water, but watched as they lined up and went about transporting the water away, shouting and waving greetings at each other.

Another line further away caught his eye, and he went to see what that one was. The people gave a uniformed man pieces of paper in return for green plastic bags of what was probably food. When he got in line, holding his breath at being so close to the others, a guy who stepped in behind him said, "Robin Hood," and snickered. Dave turned. "Oooee!" the man said, "you are ripe."

"How do I get food?" Dave asked.

"Scrip, but—" The guy squinted. "Don't you know?"

"No, I'm from way up north."

"Move on, come on," a girl behind the guy said.

Dave moved, one hand on the bike. "Really," he said to the guy. "I just got here a little while ago. Been livin'—"

"Hey clown, your turn."

"Pick up," the uniformed man said, holding his hand out without looking up.

"Uh, I don't have no things. Those little papers?"

The man sighed and looked up with bored annoyance. "Screwed yourself out so early in the week? Jesus, I can't understand how you guys can go through all this just for a little nookie. She musta been something. You gotta go to the registry."

"I never been to the registry. Supposta get free—"

"Get outta here dummy," the uniformed man said. "Next."

Dave stepped out of the line, his face hot with embarrassment. "Where's the registry?" he asked the guy behind him, who now headed off with his green bag of food. Dave got back in the line, deciding to try the uniformed man again.

"Here," a girl said. "I got you a bag." She was the one two places behind him. He recoiled at her closeness.

"Thanks," he said. The bag was small, but seemed like enough to get him to the Complex.

"You were telling the truth? You never been here before?"

"Huh? I mean, no." He backed away, his face flushed.

"Well where've you been?"

Barbara Velleli's apartment overlooks a street-corner near the entrance to the inner ring, only a kilometer or two from the West New York Gate. The apartment is rich with color, stuffed with expensive loot. Elaborately colored rugs hang on the walls and make the floors spongy. She has collected silver candelabras, statues, marble objects. She has closetfuls of food, fur coats, old paintings. While they eat their cakes, she speaks with absolute frankness about what she is doing. Five years ago, she says, she began receiving looted objects in trade for indoor humps (Huh?) that means real bedroom appointments with makeup and all, none of that baloney in the bushes. That means men with connections, with certain expectations in a girl, not simply slam bam thank you ma'am—Dave is content to sit and fails to listen completely. He has never been this close to a girl. The odors in the apartment are rife with the suggestion of a girl's lair. Every object emits a dizzying sweetness, something like the strange, almost nauseating sweetness of the roses his mother grew outside their house. And he is mesmerized by the physical closeness, watches her chest heave and deflate as she speaks, sees the slight dots of nipples in the blue sweater. She is hefty and very healthy looking and it is clear that she is doing all right. She shifts frequently in her overstuffed chair, her flesh straining against her jeans, her breasts sliding inside the heavy sweater.

"How come I get to come up here? Why did you give me food," he asks, finally.

"You're from the outside, you said. You don't know anything. I just wanted to know what's with you." She looks at him. He flushes, looks around. "Besides, you can't hurt me. I have mace." He screws his face up at her. "Yeah." She holds up a little blue can with a spray attachment on top. "One zap and your eyes are gone. You can't hurt me. Got a .38, too."

"Well I never intended to."

"Well you won't either." She smiles.

He tries to tell his story. Buffalo, life up there, the trip down. His face burns as he tells it because she watches him, leaning forward with her chin on her hand. He almost stammers, has difficulty holding himself still. The stink of his fear rises into his nostrils. Finally he says, "I got a lottery ticket."

"Don't we all," she says.

"No, a good one, a matched number."

Her response is disbelief. She checks and rechecks the numbers, then seems to become almost angered. She goes to the window to stare at the massive profile of the Complex, shaking her head slowly, muttering in amazement. He glances at the Complex too, thinks, well, I better get out of here. He rises, moves toward the door. "Wait wait," she says, turning from the window. "I'm sorry. It's just that, well, you know? You're the only person in the whole world I ever saw who has a good ticket, except in films." She points at the couch again. "Please, stay."

She continues to talk: she is twenty-two. She has enough here to almost buy that goddamned place and inside of a year she will be in it. Those other girls who do it in the bushes'll be dying at just about the time she walks through the gate. They're dirty, they don't take care of themselves, they'll spread for any dirty punk who can flash a little scrip at them. Men with connections'd never mess with those moldy little twerps. Without a reputation you're sunk. She is the best there is, the best around, because she maintains the old standards, she keeps herself fit, she knows how to please. Because she is not in the inner ring you might think she is dreaming but that's wrong. She goes there when she wants to. There are gentlemen who take care of her, who would do anything for her services. She is here because in there you can't store as she does. It is illegal, and the police check, confiscate. And oh would they just love to get their hands on what she's got.

"Next time you go, can I go with you? Hey, when is—"

"They patrol the gate only on weekends," she

says. "Why don't you stay here until then and we'll go."

He swallows, not understanding. "But, well, why do you invite me like—"

She comes over and sits down next to him on the couch. He almost shrieks and bolts for the door, but holds himself steady, barely breathing. She looks at him and catches his eyes, and he is unable to take them off the small details of her features, the little marks on her face, the soft blonde hair, the little tiny creases on her thick lips, the veins in the eyeballs, the neck which undulates as she swallows, preparing to speak: "You're luck on two feet," she says, "you're a talisman."

"A what?"

"Never mind. Just stay here, okay?" He cannot speak. She briefly touches the back of his hand with her fingers. It burns. He looks at her hand, at the offending patch of skin, thinking, this is stupid, this is death. And so close, less than arm's reach, are the shoulders, breasts, all there in such complexity of detail that he almost faints.

"Just stay here," she says. "Relax. Hey, I'll show you something," and she leaves, comes back with a bottle of dark liquid and a little glass, and pours some.

"What is it?"

"Sherry, try it." The liquid is thick, heavy with sweetness, horribly appropriate, dizzying. He has one peculiar thought, that her blood, her sweat, her saliva, must all taste just like this.

That first day, behind her door locked with a two by four bar, Dave sitting there blearily gazing at her and feeling trapped and naked, she asked him right out if he'd like to have her and he said no.

(thinking: Ronald Castle. Dave is nine, watching from a distance as Ronald lies in wait for Jeannie

Whitman, half friend, half enemy, former playmate. He sets upon her and wrestles her to the ground, and gradually convinces her that this is half wrestling match and half something else, and as she is overcome her vigorously athletic defense transforms into a limp and giggling consent, so he pulls her pants off. There are urgent, conspiratorial whispers as they do it there in the weeds and dust. Dave watches, overcome with fright at the chance Ronald is taking. The fool. It is summertime. In the distance smoke fouls the sky. In one week both of them are dead, gunned down by the men of the town, barely able to perceive through their burning eyes their own executions.)

Sitting in the apartment with the hefty girl on the couch next to him he felt pursued, felt the power of her invitation to engage in this nonsensical sacrilege. It was an interruption of his movement, a distraction of his purpose, and in the funny fog produced by the sherry he knew it was worse even than shaking the hand of the infected traveller. He tried to hold himself steady, but the eyes, the face was always there, mooning at him, smiling, revealing the perfect teeth, stretching into different expressions and showing to him the secret details of dimples at the corners of mouth, of gently stretched lip, of the watery blink of eye, with the tiny dot of white in the inner corner. And the offending hand, again placed on his until he pulled it out from under, fell on his thigh and laid there like lead.

He finally gave in, mesmerized by the stultifying sweetness of that chamber decked out with the warm-colored rugs and the silver and marble. She convinced him that it was okay, really, nothing would happen, that she would like to have his luck rub off on her ho ho ho, that her talisman would bring her good fortune and she'd probably make it in within the month if he would oblige. And so he did. She kept saying what else is there anyway? When was the last time she could do it without scrip being part of the bargain? Life's too short.

In broad daylight! In fact on the couch, only ten feet from the window which showed him, if he looked, part of the upward slope of the grey and megalithic cement mountain. That picture in the window, blocked only by the silhouette of a metal statue of a man with little wings on his heels, aggravated the sense of the dumbness of the act: he felt foolish, stupid, out of his mind. In those first minutes, reaching his hand out to naked flesh he thought, with a kind of giddy and rubber-legged pleasure, this is the end, this is death. He was stunned into a speechless cancellation of his shame by the macroscopic detail of her body, the ample tit with the little curly hairs here and there around the nipple catching the sunlight in amber reflection, the tiny dark moles, the belly-button hidden down somewhere in a hole which looked like the inner cone of a flower, and below that, hidden down there between the pale and heavy thighs—all of it moved, seethed, flexed. She showed him now, although he already knew from observation, and the feeling was one of being submerged in hot fluid, but only for a second, because he was finished right at the start, limp and without tension anywhere in his body, still goggle-eyed at the closeness of that rich flesh. And she laughed, said, hang on a while honey, you're okay, what I got was okay, you'll do fine. And the second time he understood what all the fuss was about, understood how this could survive as a commodity, a valuable asset, probably one of the last things around worth selling or buying. Ceph didn't destroy the value of this although it may have destroyed the value of gold, cars, beautiful buildings. He even saw how this could be preferred over food.

He remained there the four days in a state of subtle shock, or he would sometimes broodingly think, a state of infection, of willingly derailed purpose. If she wasn't 'showing him something else' (lie still, I won't bite it), she was asking him to wash her back, give her a rubdown, usually with her lying on her back limp and spreadeagled with her eyes closed and a slight smile on her face while he moved soft and hot handfuls of flesh on her frame. He would only get half way before saying "Uh, maybe—" and she would say, "Go ahead, go ahead, you only live once." She produced foods he did not believe existed. Canned peaches impressed him the most. She gave him little strange looking brown strips of hard and chewy material which he was working on when she told him it was dried beef, and he spat it out. Meat. The thought of the fibre of a creature that died years ago nauseated him, and she laughed, tearing at the stuff herself. He thought: Vienna sausages is the same. He tried again. Was this a horse? A cow? A cow, she said. Later she would have him back on the bed again, ordering him to do something else completely outrageous: go ahead, it doesn't taste that bad, and again in macroscopic detail he sat naked on his knees and looked right down between her legs as she waited, the heavy thighs flexing, the plump swath of crotch soft and inert, and she reached out and grabbed his hand and pulled it there, saying see? go ahead, see what it's made of, don't be so shy.

He refused to sleep with her at night in the bed. He lay in his bag, awake, staring at the ceiling or at the twinkling lights of the Complex, overcome with subtle fear. He was locked in the chamber, breathing the tainted air. No breeze blew here, there was no moist coolness in the morning, and if he slept, he awoke feeling drugged and sick from the thick and awful sweetness of the air which lay still on him like a slab of light jelly. He got diarrhea, ended up in the middle of the night in her 'bathroom', a back room in one of the empty apartments at the back of the building. She somehow had got ahold of about a half a ton of bagged "Kitty Kleen" cat litter from some warehouse, and stored it in the room. She would put it in a wide pail with a toilet seat on top, and empty it into the alley behind the building whenever it became saturated. Four storeys down, in the back alley was a huge mound of used litter, the walls of surrounding buildings heavily dusted with it. He would stumble back, his rear end burning, and crawl into the false safety of his bag, the sweat of his fear beading on his face—diarrhea is a germ! The perfect host. I got to get out of here. But there was no place to go. He had to wait it out, try to sleep, try to forget that he was hopelessly closed in.

She told him he smelled funny and made him wash himself, strictly forbidden according to the book: *don't rub off, for any reason, the oil of the skin—it is produced for a reason, and too much soap or abrasive cleaners make it vulnerable.* But he gave in anyway. What possible help could the skin be now? After what he had done with this girl? The violation was so complete that he felt as if he had not only wallowed on the surface of the rich fat of the girl's body, but he had squirmed, penetrated and wallowed in and around organs, viscera, blood-crimson membranes, inner oils, secret tubes and chambers, rich and viscous mucous and hot, virulent clots of germs. And those horribly and powerfully sweet foods which made him shudder and almost swoon with revulsion, but which he could not resist, violated his insides, suffused him with infection. He was doomed.

She showed him little heavy bars she said was gold, other little bars of silver. Old currency which she said would be worth something some day. She also showed him a valuable collection of old postage stamps, with the rich, minute engraving similar to that on the currency. He spent long periods of time leafing through the heavy volumes containing the stamps. She had a huge collection of sealed bottles of pills, different kinds of drugs, powders, sealed cans of marijuana.

Outdoors the nights were the same as his first. Below her window and all along the street there were sounds of violence, there were fires, shadows of people trading things, girls making deals with groups of men. At any time he went to the window he would hear impressive things: below and to the left, a scream, choked off. He looks—hunched shadows move on bricks. Yes, apparently it is a girl being raped. Fool, she shouldn't have gone out. She protests violently, and then finally wimpers, and the only sounds after that are arguments about who is next. A drunk staggers along, wasted on the experimental chem lab brew of the cellars of these buildings, shouting out his anger and hopelessness. Thugs do not bother to sack him. Beyond this glitter a few electric lights of some of the buildings in the inner ring. He hears no sounds from there, because the closer sounds of violence and hellraising obscure them. Up in the smoky mist, in the blackness, he gets a vague sense of the mammoth shape of the Complex by the twinkling of lights which appear something like stars. Sometimes these lights disappear into the mist and the only sight beyond the barb wire fence is the flickering of fires from the inner ring. He listens: someone is being beaten up just below the window. He hears his head slap the pavement, the muffled sounds of kicks. Barbara, wearing only black lace underpants, goes to the window, her thighs caressing each other with each languid step. She carries with her a plate of fruit cocktail, and looks out over the street. The silhouette of her heavy breast hangs in the window frame. "Filthy pigs," she says, and returns to the couch, sits, and reclines in his lap. There is nothing else to do. He places his hand on her belly and slides it inside the pants. Below, the sounds of the man being beaten continue.

At other times Dave would stand at the window and look down to the street as Barbara emerged from the building, wearing a trenchcoat and carrying a package. She would cross the street, wait near a fire, one hand in her pocket on the cocked .38. Two or three men would join her and they would negotiate angrily for five minutes. She always held firm, frequently pointed up to the window where Dave stood resisting the urge to go to the bathroom. Finally she would give them the package in return for slips of paper, miner's points usually, useless since she is not registered, but the next thing to hard currency anytime she needs anything from a miner. The little certificates were the official looking green and black similar to the lottery tickets and the old currency.

Protection of her belongings was a problem, she explained. Mr. Maresca, who acted as owner and guard of her building, watched over when she was gone, in return for food, and once in a while, when she saw that he could become greedy enough to appropriate her loot, she invited him up to her place for some good wine, food, and a first class piece of ass. He would have to cross her only once to lose the best.

Throughout the days approaching the weekend Dave wandered around the apartment or looked at the stamp books, stood in the food lines with her or sat and ate peaches, those sickly sweet violaters of his insides which he could not resist, frequently found himself lazily recognizing the first signs of this peculiar, apparently ceaseless lust which she was always so willing to satisfy with a kind of placid and luscious submission. With all this came the vague but increasing wish to either take her with him or stay, and he would immediately throw the idea out as too dangerous, and the second he thought that he would again think of the tantalizing alternative to fleeing to the aseptic safety of the Complex: the clean and naked body of the girl there whenever he wanted it. Each time he broke through the gentle, dry resistance of her with that first push and slid into the liquid heat of her body, sometimes watching himself passing into her under the curly mound, he thought that this was as far as he ever needed to come, that any more was excess, that even if he lived only a couple of years doing this, then he would have lived a good life. When he was through he would glimpse through the window that section of upward slope, grey and mammoth, and tick off in his mind the remainder of time he had to wait to get to it and safety. The nullification of lust, of course, immediately brought back his reason.

He asked her when she planned to try to get in.

"It's a matter of developing the right contacts," she said, "it might happen any time, it might never happen."

"It's almost better here," he said. "I almost wish—"

"Listen, there're lots of other girls in there too. Besides, you can't stay here. You're eating up all my food."

"I know, I know."

"If you feel like staying another week—"

He looked through the window. "No, I can't."

"I suppose not," she said, looking at the window. A shadow crossed her face, a strange look that seemed to indicate a hatred for what she saw. "I guess I'd start walking right now if—" She threw up her hands. "Well, anyway, want some fruit?"

His mouth watered. "No," he said, feeling a peculiar, gurgling warning from his stomach, "well, yeah, yeah, I'll have some."

And so the day comes. Barbara makes her preparations early in the morning while Dave sits at the window and watches the doings of the people. Bums stagger by. Upstairs windows open and out comes the yell, "Heads up" and then pots of brownish yellow liquid mixed with human waste are emptied into the street in long, graceful arcs, so that large, black splats can be seen all along the sidewalks. Women lug their water pails around, headed for the food lines, laughing and talking on the way.

Barbara is taking some "big C" to a "farm exec" in the inner ring. Her John, she says, was an old friend of her father's and runs a couple of south Jersey truck farms from his mansion in the inner ring. He makes frequent trips into the Complex. Spends most of his time in quarantine, otherwise does business in there. He is rich, powerful, and when Dave asks, why her? she explains as follows: he is a kink and she will spend the weekend being his patient lying on a doctor's examination table, she will fight him off as he rapes her, she will be an overfed preteener who knows nothing about sex who gets it from all angles in the guise of some East Indian contortion lesson from a lecherous master who somehow hides his true intent until she finds him buried to the hilt and studiously attempting to rationalize this, too, as another part of the lesson. For this relationship to remain stable, and old family ties help, she must maintain her somewhat hefty physique because he always said that he likes nothing more than "girls who always complain that they are on the thin edge of losing their battles with advancing weight." She fits the bill, Dave notices. She bulges, just enough. When she fiddles with her dirty blonde hair, arms up, there is the ample expanse of plump underarm, shoulder, and majestic, uplifted breasts. She exudes the aura of corruption by plenty and more important, possesses this impossible richness of flesh, perfect skin, impressive mammary heft, in an age of starvation and certain death. Her existence alone, Dave sees, is a defiance of reality, and gives anyone who is lucky enough to have her a kind of nonsensical hope.

"What's the big C?"

"Cocaine—it's hard to get inside. But anybody can give him that. I give him memories of the old days. He likes me because I'm a good actor."

"What's that got to—"

"Well, I know how to act ignorant and shy. He's an awful guy too. Got this drawer full of junk that he—"

"Like what?"

She snickers. "Never mind. None of your business anyway. He's just a freak about things that work by batteries."

"Like what?"

"Come on, come on, we gotta go."

Downstairs they are stopped by Mr. Maresca. He is a gaunt, balding man in a sleeveless tee shirt. He looks at her. "I watch," he says. "No sweat kid. I'll keep the punks out."

"Thanks."

"And there're a lot of 'em around, honey," he says, leering. "Last night, Christ, I had to about fight them hand to hand."

"Okay, okay," she says. "Monday all right? I'm not back till Sunday night. Monday."

"Sure kid, just come downstairs."

"No, you come to my place."

"No, downstairs this time. You hardly ever seen my place."

"Okay."

"And who's this?"

"A friend, just a friend."

Approaching the break in the barb wire fence: "Don't say anything," she says. "Let me do the talking. These guys are creeps.'' The uniformed soldiers elbow their shoulder slung automatic weapons behind them. One recognizes Barbara.

''Baby,'' he says, ''vacationing in funland this weekend?''

''I have a package to take through,'' she says. ''What's the going rate?''

He chuckles, shrugs. ''Well, if there was time we'd have some suggestions.'' The other guard laughs. ''But since we don't, how's about a few points?''

''Scrip.''

''C'mon, I can paper my walls with that stuff. Points would be better. What's carrying?''

''Coke.''

''Well,'' and he muses, talking with his eyes to the other guard. ''Well well well, no sense in causing trouble for travellers. We'll each take a fifty.'' She shakes her head. ''We will,'' he says, ''or you won't go through. And you gotta be going somewhere specific. Come curfew time—''

''I'm going somewhere specific,'' she says. ''Twenty apiece, and I don't wanna push, but someone's waiting for me, and if I don't show your ass is grass.''

''Who's the big deal?''

''Why don't you make a guess?''

''Well,'' and he shrugs. She gives them the certificates. ''Hey, can we search you?'' All three guffaw.

''Some time when I need a favor you can come over to my place and search all you want.''

''Okay, we'll remember. We know where you chicks hide all your goodies.''

''But no fooling. You stay my friends and you'll be okay. You mess, and some men in grey suits are going to be very unhappy with you.''

''And who's this?''

''He comes with me.''

The man shakes his head. ''Rules is rules. No

amount of paper helps here. It's been hot for too long. Shouldn't even let you through actually. People are on edge." She pauses, looks at the profile of the Complex, and sighs.

"Show him." Dave leans his bike against his side and draws out his papers. Both guards look, cross check the numbers, look at his face, look at each other. They scheme with their eyes.

"No funny stuff," Barbara says.

"Nah, no use to me."

When they are through he sees that her upper lip is beaded with sweat, her face is lined with worry. She seems distracted, strange, alone.

The panorama changes inside the wire. The first thing he sees is a jeep going by with a roar. The streets are clean, the buildings better kept up. "The West Gate is right ahead about a kilometer and a half. Nobody'll bother you on the way. Just go to the gate and follow the signs."

He looks at the Complex. From here it looks less like a mountain than from a distance, because some of the higher stacks of chambers are obscured by the new perspective.

"I just don't understand the fence," he says.

"Remember? This is the legitimate subordinate population. Outside are people who came during the migrations. That was when the fence was built, to keep the sick out, protect the stuff stored here. They allow some travel in, but you gotta have papers to live here. They check all the time." She looks around at the buildings. "You know that this place is filled with stuff from museums all over the country? All kinds of rare things are kept around here."

He nods, looking around. "Well," she says, "it's been fun. It's nice to have someone to talk to." She looks again at the Complex, her eyes searching the domes, portholes. Distracted, she shakes her head, then sighs quickly. "Okay, I hope you make it quick.

I'll be seeing you inside in a couple of months."

"Can— Is there anything I can do?"

"Yes. I have a note here with addresses. This one," and she pulls it out of her pocket, "is Stephen Breen. He's the farm exec. If you contact him or he contacts you, he'll have something you can do for him and me. In fact, I'm arranging that this weekend. If you can just, well, do a couple of things, whatever he tells you you *can* do, then maybe I'll have a better chance." She pauses, smiles. "You know I don't do for anybody else what I did for you."

He sees it in a little flash. There was a reason all along. "You're some girl," he says.

She laughs. "If I get in then you can have anything you want. Know what I mean?"

"Sure. I'll do what I can."

"That's what I was hoping."

"Actually you make it kinda hard for me to go. I wish you could come."

"Oh I'll get there," she says, nodding with a kind of scheming conviction. "Don't worry. I'm playing this game better than anybody I know—I got enough now to *waltz* in. I just need somebody to make arrangements."

"I— It's kinda awful, what you gotta do. Those guys at the wire, that slimy Mr. Whatsisname. You gotta—"

"Honey, it's my business to know how to handle them."

"Well it's kinda awful."

"They know where the best is. Why would they mess with the best? All they got left is the little skinny ones in the bushes, the ones they call slit. They never call *me* that."

"I wish—"

"Never mind, I got plenty going. Just remember me, okay?"

"Okay." She looks at the Complex again, and that shadow crosses her face. She seems unsure now. She looks at it with a mixture of lust and hatred, and over all of that, she looks unconvinced of all she says about her chances. The clarity, the simple truth of what is now going to happen makes clear to him the distraction and strange hopelessness on her face: he is going into the Complex, straight ahead. She is veering off to go into some building somewhere around here, to present herself to the hands and eyes of a dirtyminded kink who, powerful as he is, cannot live in the Complex either.

III

The separation from Barbara makes him feel without substance, an isolated vacuum. He rides along slowly, watching the cement fringe of the Complex enlarge before him. He thinks of her making deals with leering men, and the mysterious horror of it makes his throat knot. He goes into an archway. It becomes a low ceilinged tunnel of raw cement with the same sign every thirty meters: "Present Verification at Window. Unauthorized Persons Keep Out. Caution: Do Not Tamper With Ceiling Gas Jets." He looks up. Every few meters there are small nipples of metal protruding from the cement.

The man inside the window seems suspended under water—the glass is thick, appears blue green in tint, and as Dave moves his head laterally the man's image moves with it.

"I have a matching lottery ticket and ID number," he says into the little metal grille.

The voice that speaks back is flat, distant. "Place the papers into the slot at the left." He does so, and the figure moves around and peers into a television screen, pauses, turns back. The papers reappear in the slot.

"Please wait," the voice says. Dave looks around. There is no place to sit, and he feels vaguely frightened at being in such close quarters. Anybody could just press a button and start the jets. He backs away from the window, seeing the figure disappear into a small archway.

He waits twenty minutes, frequently sighs, returns to the window to peer in at the contents of the booth. Chair, desk, little TV screen. Nothing else, no pictures on the walls, no plants. This would be the outer underside of the Complex. Beyond the window it might take half a day to get to the bright middle.

Still he feels strange and substanceless. He does not want to go in. Foolish, he knows, but the thought returns again and again: things that work with batteries. It is horrible, the thought of that awful man leering and pushing her into strange contortions while she is forced to play act like a child. And those rotten soldiers, what would they do? The whole thing is unbelievably wretched—she does not deserve it, does not deserve having that fat, pale delicacy violated again and again.

The man returns. Dave goes to the window, listens.

"The authenticity of the certificate must be verified. Please come back one week from today. Bring no personal effects."

Dave leans down. "Listen, they're good. What's the trouble? Why can't they check them out now?"

"We must check photostats. Verification takes time."

"Why a week?"

"Please return in a week," the flat voice says.

"That's not legal. I wanna come in. You can't keep me from coming in. Read the certificate."

"Return in a week," the voice says, and before retiring to his anteroom, he says, "Take the pink slip from the slot. It will provide temporary residence."

Dave speaks on, leaning down to the little grille: "This is not legal. It says I am guaranteed entry."

The bluegreen window turns black, a deep, bottomless watery black. He pulls the pink slip from the slot. He turns to leave and sees a man walking in his direction, carrying an attache case. He backs off and watches. The man looks at him as he passes, suspicious of the bicycle and the curved bow ends sticking up like horns above the pack tied to the handlebars.

The man goes to the window, slides a card in the slot. The window lights, the man speaks softly into the grille, leaning over so as not to permit Dave to hear. Then, ten feet down from the window, there is a loud hiss, and part of the wall appears as a square which turns to permit the man to go through. When Dave returns to the window, it is the same velvet black as before. He waits, looks at the slip. There is an address, and next week's appointment time written on the bottom. He shrugs and leaves.

"Let's see the slip."

"It'll only be a week. The voice said a week. Next Saturday I go for an interview."

The man guffaws. "Sure kid. Well, come on in. I'll show you your new home."

It is on the fourth floor, a small combination bedroom and living room. The toilet is a pot which he can empty into a kind of coal shute out one of the back windows.

"What about food?"

"Oh, just come down to number five. We got that set up as a lounge. Got the fish patties and other stuff, soft drinks. We sit around and talk."

"Who else stays here?"

"People like yourself. Plaintiffs. We're all in court cases. We're the ones whose certificates were stolen, or who lost birth records, or who had our names used by false entrants. Court cases take a long time." The man nods, thinking. "But you got this slip here, and it means you should have immediate entry." And then he adds, "Providing they don't close off the sectors."

"Why would they do that?"

"Each sector is a quarter kilometer square—you wouldn't know it any other time except summer, when the weather gets bad, like now. This week they got two cases down a way. So they're worried."

"This sector borders the Complex?"

"No. It's one over. Say, what took you so long?"

"Well, we lived okay for all the years, up in Buffalo."

"Buffalo, New York?" the man says, squinting, "not just hustling on the outside?"

"No, been livin' up there all this time. Just came down last week."

"Through all the outside stuff?"

Yeah, through all of it. Killed one guy up in Waldwick, one way up in Utica. Took a long time—

He seems to have repeated this many times, but here he is again later in the day in the lounge, and the people sit chins on fists, and stare at him as he tells of his journey into the inner ring. The refugees, eating their patties, sitting close enough to indicate that they feel little immediate fear of the Ceph, casually exchange short sentences until someone else says shh, and Dave's face burns with shyness as he raps out the incidents in short sentences. They do not know that you can live off the land. It has not occurred to them. They had assumed, everyone had assumed, that living outside any of the rings meant certain death, that without medicated food there was too much vulnerability.

The four girls in the group of nine remain silent and watch, and each time his eyes meet with the glance of one of them he burns again, recalling Barbara and catching himself before glancing between their denimclad legs and at their various sized tits. Because of Barbara, every girl is suddenly a being with infinite possibilities, with secrets, inner sexual mysteries, all of which now have a suddenly discovered use, application to him. It is the *idea* of cunt, the understanding of its specific relationship to him, that makes him glance and immediately speculate. Therefore he stammers, flushes whenever one looks at him, because his mind's vision is now infected with an imaginary X-ray capacity which sees only sexual equipment.

The five men in the group are all older than Dave. One has gray hair and is called Mr. Kellner, and he is interested mainly in how they lived in Buffalo without dying of the Ceph. "It's not supposed to be possible," he says. "You're saying you never once took any other precaution but the ones you mentioned, just that stuff your father told you in the book?"

"Yeah, in fact I'd still be there if'n it hadnabeen for 'at fella the traveller."

"Amazing," a girl cackles, "I don't believe that accent."

Dave blushes, and Mr. Kellner looks at the girl and says, "Doreen, please, you're embarrassing the boy."

Day by day the dialogue continues, now with Dave learning of the multitude of tribulations those filing suit have gone through trying to get the illegal entrants who have gone in their places. He finds that the average age of the people living in the building is about twenty-five. They were all robbed, except for

Herb Kellner, who was the last anyone knew of to come to the Complex with a good ticket, seven years ago, arriving on foot, but he did not have any certificate proving his identity because that was lost before he made the trip, and some other crafty bastard somehow altered his own lottery ticket to fool the authorities and get into Herb's place. The authorities know who he is, but loopholes in the law get him stays, get Kellner's various appeals nullified, and so forth. The younger ones are trying to go to court against those who, years ago, stole all their identification and entered without a hitch, and their suits have been going on for six years in some cases. The pessimists in the group, about half, mostly male, believe that the only reason the government lets them carry on with their suits is that they must appear to care about the plight of the dying outside. Dave recognizes that that which they lust to get into, they would as soon blow up. They see conspiracies against them, see the illegal entrants paying off officials, they regard themselves as honest people deprived of their legal rights by red tape, by political expediency, by a refusal on the part of the officials to admit that they could make a mistake. Dave also realizes that these people are the cream of the hopefuls, are in better shape, in a way, than Barbara's farm exec, whose trips inside are only business visits and cannot be extended. Of course he might buy his way in tomorrow, but actually has less right than these people. When Dave speaks during these discussions, he usually asks only one question: why don't they just let you in?

It is Herb Kellner who comes out with the strangest answer: we are the symbols of the hopeful. We have our rights, and someday, it is guaranteed, they will be acknowledged. If they were now, then this house would have to be filled with more hopefuls of some sort, or the poor losers on the outside wouldn't be able to see anyone who is right on the thin edge of walking through the hissing door. Don't you see? It's all a joke. Every sector has people like us. We'll never get in, because out here we perform a more important function, to take the air out of revolution. Our suits will go on for eternity because if we either won or were rejected for good then everybody else around here would suddenly see just how big that mined apron really is. I don't know why they don't just come out and do what they'd really like to do, just spray all of us to death and get clean of the Ceph and the subordinate population in one shot.

"You're really way off!" a girl yells. "You always talk like that! You try to make it sound as if there wasn't any hope at all! Why don't you just keep quiet? Just for a day or so, huh?"

"There *is* no hope," he says, "it's just that you're too young to see that."

"You're too old to see that there *is*."

"Ignorance that comes from long experience, eh? Hahaha."

"Christ!" she shrieks, and stalks out.

"What got into her?" Kellner says to one of the men.

"Everybody's on edge, Herb. It's the weather, the weather."

"Ah, of course. Anyway," he says to Dave, "next time one of us makes it and all the stuff is properly verified, it'll be on TV and a big thing will be made of it. Point is that when one gets in, a little part of every one of the rest goes with them, sighs with relief. All is right with the world, the mighty wheels of Complex justice creak along, we're not just being waited out, which ought to be obvious to everyone. See, if the death rate continues like it has for another generation, then there's a good chance that all of us'll go. All it takes is some bad weather."

People sigh, snort with disagreement, try to initiate

softer discussions on other subjects elsewhere in the room. Then, silence. Dave sees it in their faces. Their eyes dart around into the corners of the room, their hands move with mindless compulsion. They are afraid to the pits of their beings.

"The population is allowed to increase at more than a one to one level in there!" Kellner shouts, sending a crumb from his fishcake arcing through the air, "don't you see the effects of that?"

"That's hearsay," someone drones.

"What's the one to one thing?" Dave asks.

"Why does that thing expand all the time?" Kellner says. "People die, you know. It expands to accomodate the increase in the population inside. Not new tennis courts, football fields."

"Don't listen to the old kook."

"Think about it," Kellner says, squinting at Dave, "why does it expand? Why can't we just go inside if it keeps getting bigger?"

It all gives Dave a headache. He cannot believe that people have such a capacity to talk. Part of it, he knows, is that for them speech is nervous release. It is the bad weather.

During the times he is not sitting listening to Kellner's rantings and the stories of the others, he walks around in the moist, late summer heat. It is not like Buffalo weather. The air here seems almost like a jelly, fouled by the smoke of the fires and the peculiar, soft pungency of whatever it is that belches out of the cement mountain on days when the wind blows west. In the old days this weather forewarned outbreaks, although here he cannot imagine such a thing happening. The streets are too clean, the Complex too close, and Saturday, when the gate will open again, looms closer and closer. Once inside all he will have to worry about is colds.

But the secret, pessimistic corner of his mind is at work. At night, alone in his bag, wide-eyed in the breezeless chamber, the fear creeps in, and he begins to moan softly and rock back and forth as he had done so many times in the woods. This time it is not the boredom, it is the powerful sensation of being hopelessly closed in and vulnerable. The last major outbreak was late July of last year, they said. Heat and moist stillness were responsible, they said. And here the same conditions are repeated. He imagines pools of hot, stinking water in marshes breeding germs. He sees people seething in their own dirty, acid sweat, and somewhere in there, secretly at work, is the beginning of the parasitic process, the refugee germ travelling along, eyes wide for opportunity, striking when the first chance at a host comes along. And in how many people at once? The terrible possibilities inherent in geometric progression, the pingpong ball sitting on the set rat trap. And then there would be the useless defensive response, ahh don't worry, it's just a cold, just need some vitamin C and I'll be okay. And the dupe: these people here, living in these drastically close quarters, fail at half of their acts to honor the code of caution. Charlie would go mad in this, he thinks. He wouldn't last a day. Even Dave, better than Charlie at honoring the code, has committed sacrilege on the grand scale and knows he might pay for it. For this reason he has been instituting reform and will not sit closer than eight feet away from anyone. But somewhere in his body, already, maybe finding its way into him from somewhere in the subterranean depths of the glutinous and seething pulp of Barbara Velelli's body, is the young and hopeful germ looking for a host in which to multiply itself in trillions. He is now astonished at himself for having done it, but understands his rashness, because he sometimes knows beyond doubt that death by the germ is inevitable and the Complex is a plastic and cement dream. He also knows that this belief is counterfeit, experimental, and permits himself to play on it only because of his closeness to being admitted.

Walking, gazing from less than a kilometer at the massive structure, he shakes his head and feels that strange, inert and relaxed acceptance of death by Ceph, so much so that he is not bothered by Saturday's rejection, which is receding in his mind as the new Saturday approaches. He has managed to last so long that the string of experiences behind him diving back into the early days of fires and flying bullets seems an eternity, and he feels old, in a way worn out.

Fear invades him at night, and when he talks to the others, and is heightened when a case of the Ceph is reported by word of mouth Friday morning, only two sectors away to the south. Their eyes dart around the candlelit room. Us next? Two sectors away? They seek security in talk. They begin to repeat themselves in their stories about the conspiracies against them. The optimists continue with their cases for the rights of the Complex authorities, but now with sweat beading their faces. Herb Kellner continues with his one monotonous rhetorical question, why don't they just let us in? Dave thinks, today, then Saturday.

His almost exasperatingly boring wait for the moment of return to the Complex is interrupted: a blond haired man wearing a kind of scientist's smock stands in the front doorway of the house and informs him that Mr. Breen would like to see him immediately, if possible. Dave turns and looks back down the hallway at the house manager's door, which has just closed.

"Don't worry about him," the man says, "officials are showing up here all the time."

"Do I hafta go?"

"Of course not. Mr. Breen said something about how you were in a position to help out a certain girl, that's all. He just wants to talk."

"Okay."

"We'll walk—you don't need anything. Be back long before curfew."

Dave shrugs and follows him. It is a fast, four hundred yard walk, and half way they pass through the open gate into the last quarter kilometer square sector before the Complex. Dave feels an eerie fear about going out of his sector, because of the case reported two sectors south. Any movement which interrupts his deliberate waiting for Saturday morning seems dangerous and unnecessary.

The building has a small sign above the door reading "Federal Hydroponics Project". The man in the smock leads him through a large, low ceilinged room with little glassed in offices, each with a person inside. They type, sit at their desks talking on phones, talk in low tones in twos.

The man tells him to go inside and sit down, and indicates a door at the end of a long hall in back of the staff's room. The sensation of peculiar anger rises into his throat as he approaches the door and opens it. Things that work with batteries, he thinks.

Stephen Breen sits behind a huge, ornate desk, and behind him the walls are decorated with expensive looking artifacts similar to the ones Barbara had in her place. The office is dim and stuffy with collected junk, like a museum. Breen himself is a greyhaired man with very pink skin and eyes so bloodshot that he looks as if he has the bug. "Uh, the guy tol' me to—"

"Siddown," he says. He continues to look at Dave as if he is thinking vaguely of some other subject more important than his presence. "Let me ask you one question," he says, "Barb says you lived without medicated food. Is that true?"

"Yeah." He looks around. "Is she here?"

"No no, she can't stay here—not even supposed to be here, but I arranged—" He looks vaguely at the wall to the left of his desk. "Splendid girl," he says softly.

"What's hydroponic mean?"

"Huh? Oh, hydroponic, hydroponic. That means growing things without soil. That's what we do, grow stuff without soil, in nutritive water. Down south outside the population, in huge greenhouses. Have our own little army, have our own little border wars with people who want the food—"

"Punks."

"That's them," he says, nodding vaguely. He becomes silent for a moment, looking at his desk, then jerks his body to a kind of sitting attention, saying, "okay, okay. Barb tells me you can be trusted not to blab things around to people. Is that true?"

"Yeah, I guess so."

"Well, as I said, pure food is my business, but we do a little side stuff as well. A little moonlighting, you might call it. And what I need is a new sort of courier for my products, see? I could carry the stuff in, but the heat's on in there. Funny, you'd think that they wouldn't bother with the old laws once the bug hit, but they do, they surely do." He pauses, turns in his chair, and his face is suddenly lined with a kind of melancholy worry, as if what he wants from Dave won't help his situation any. He opens a drawer and brings out a green flask with a yellow label. "This is Cutty, boy. Twenty five years old. Want some?"

"Nope. Listen, it's gonna get dark, an' I gotta—"

"Relax," he says, taking a swig from the bottle. "No problem, no problem. As I was saying—"

"Yeah, this product thing."

"Right, products products. All right—I'm in the junk business see? I once was an honest businessman, but now I'm in the junk business. I can grow the best food around, the richest tomatoes, the best brocolli, but no, what they want from me is the best heroin, the finest coke, and it seems now that that's what I do. I'm in the junk business and I can't get out of it and I got a bad liver and I'm sick. I'm getting sicker and sicker and if I can't get inside that place soon then somebody else'll have to take over my junk business, see?"

"Yeah—"

"—because there are a lot of heavy habits in there, see? Lots of people need my junk and there's no place else they can get it. Oh, maybe. I mean there are other farms, other sick bagmen all over I suppose, but we got a lot of heavy habits to take care of in there, we gotta produce, busy busy busy—" and he bursts out laughing, and ends up rubbing his eyes and shaking his head in a kind of humorous exasperation. "—busy busy. Yeah."

"What about Barbara?"

"Yes yes, we're working on that, we're working. I'm trying to arrange for both of us—"

"She's got a lot of stuff too, you know. In her place."

"Stuff?"

"Statues and stamps and little bars of gold and stuff."

Breen laughs. "Oh lord," he says, "oh lord. Young people—how misled they—That stuff is worth nothing. Not a cent." He thinks, squints at his desk. "Worthless, worthless. *Any*way, you got a ticket to go in, scot free. And this business of living without medicated food, that's what they are interested in, and that's what interests me, see? My former contacts are heavy medical officials, from up center."

"Up center?"

"From the research labs, up there where the legislative personnel live. Very restricted. Impervious. Almost nobody allowed in there. People who pull the strings, see? And here I am, poor, sick, rotten livered bagman—been doing this for them for years with the understanding that eventually, well," and he trails off again, gesturing at the wall with a hopeless flap of his hand. "Something is rotten in the state of Denmark," he says.

"Denmark?" Dave screws his face up at the man.

"I mean something's just not right any more. Not right. Must be too much heat in there or something. I'm taking a big chance with you boy, a big chance. Like, it's coming to the last gasp and all. This is all very dangerous for me, very. I wish I could really trust you."

"You can," he says. "I mean, what am I supposed to do?"

"Look, I can call in to my doctor friends in there, but I can't say anything about our little arrangement—security is really tight, as they say. No code, nothing. I have to be able to transfer information to them, and you're it. So I call in and say that I know of a guy who lived without medicated food, right? Well, my doctor friend will naturally want to know just how the hell you did that, and when you get there, you can also say that Mr. Breen wants to talk to him about other matters. See?"

"Barbara said you could go into the Complex any time."

"I can go into the quarantine sections for various reasons, like medical treatment, like routine checks of food service maintenance. But I can't go up center for sure." He stares at the wall again, thinking. "We'll just see—we'll just see how this strikes my friends in the medical profession. You just tell them that it has become necessary for me to communicate with them. They'll use you for that. Some ruse to get you to be able to float between up center and the quarantine sectors, something like that. Then they'll get word to me. They oughtta be getting heat from their clients soon, cause their clients can't legislate and cold turkey at the same time," and he bursts out laughing again, this time seemingly losing control, his hands on his face. When he finishes, he rubs his face slowly but forcefully so that his skin goes from its normal pink to a deep red. "Oh lord," he says. "Things are certainly going down hill."

"I don't see how it'd be so hard for you to arrange to meet them in quarantine yourself."

"True, it does seem easy, but there are a lot of straights in there who run things, and they got this security system, and they know I have vast fields of poppies and coca brush inside my inflatable greenhouses. They must. Maybe they don't, I don't know," and he trails off again, waving his hand at a window on the Complex side of his office. "I even got some pioneers who set up coca brush down in Virginia, know that? Salvaged punks. Used to be we just blew them away, but we salvaged some and made a little army of Johnny Appleseeds out of them. With a little rudimentary education about how to harvest, zap, I got a big junk business."

Dave is not sure he understands what Breen is telling him. He thinks, tries to put it all together in his mind one more time. "Okay, you say I don't hafta do anything. Not anything at all?"

"Only one thing," he says. "One doctor will spend a lot of time interviewing you about living without medicated food, okay? He's one of the heavy researchers, one of the guys whose job it is to crack the bug before all of us die. He would be one of four researchers who are on the other end of my business. After he asks about survival techniques for a while, you'll know he's not after routine stuff like blood tests and that. He's the one to ask the following: 'Mr. Breen would like to discuss other matters too.' Got it?"

"How's he supposed to know it's the, uh, junk business."

"He will, he will. See, I'm getting the silent

treatment. Must be the weather. Everything goes wrong in summer, no one's really himself, see? We all get a little batshit in summer," and he laughs again. "Yeah, batshit, that's what we get. It's the bug, the bug. Any year now—"

"They said there was a case a few sectors over."

Breen sighs, looks distractedly at his desk. "It's never your own sector, but it's always only a few away. Who's they?"

"I don't know."

"Listen, you really going to do this for me?"

"Will I get in trouble?"

"Not if you keep your mouth shut. I wish I could trust you to—"

"Don't worry about that. I won't tell anybody."

"I mean nobody. This is all for one researcher."

"What's his name?"

Breen looks at him again, thinking. "I don't want to confuse you. Okay, Thurston, Keene, Orlev, or McPherson. Can you remember that?" He repeats the names again, slowly. Dave ends up nodding, fixing the names in his mind. "One of those four. If it's not one of those four, then the guy won't know what you're talking about."

"How does this help Barbara?"

"I don't really know yet. I really don't know. Only that if there's one person I ever get the chance to help, it'll be her. I'm serious," and he nods with conviction slowly, still with that distracted look on his face. "It'll be her."

"Well, okay, I'll try. Long's I won't get in trouble."

Breen waves his hand at him, indicating that there isn't any chance, and goes for his little green bottle again. "It's interesting though," he says, "how one can live without the medicated food. They'll be interested in that." He begins to rise from his chair, but teeters before standing, so that he must grip the edge of the desk to steady himself.

"You okay?" Dave asks.

"No," he says. "No, not at all." He laughs again, testing his balance as he stands. "I won't try to see you to the door—"

" 's okay, it's right here."

Breen laughs again. "Right, you're right. There it is. It *is* right there. Well. Anyway—" and he looks at the window on the Complex side of the office, "anyway, let's hope we live another year," he says. "Another month, who knows—we're either back to the old grind, busy busy busy, or we're bones." He pauses again, then snorts. "Maybe I been at this too long. Seen too many people die, I guess."

"Well," Dave says, backing toward the door, "I'll see what I can do."

"Thanks son," Breen says. "Appreciate it. Barb too. I realize you wouldn't be doing this if you didn't— Well, if you didn't sort of have some feeling for her." Dave flushes at the familiarity of the statement.

"Well, I don't know—"

"She's a great girl. Wasn't for her I'd be in the rubber room by now."

"Okay, see you then."

"Yessir, if the weather holds. If the weather holds."

It is early evening by the time he returns to his house, and he realizes with a certain tingling expectation, only hours now before going into the Complex. In the lounge the plaintiffs continue at their conspiracy invention, their shadows flickering on the walls with the flames of the candles, and with Dave's arrival they turn to him, desperate for a new topic. They ask to see Charlie's book again, pump Dave for information. As he continues to tell of the fires, the bullets, he holds clean a little section in the corner of his mind which repeats Thurston, Keene, Orlev, McPherson. His nerves feel irritated to the point of exhaustion with talk, the muscles in his face feel overworked and tight from the effort that comes with the endless, repetitious formation of words. As he talks the book passes from one person to another, each of whom tips it into the candlelight and squints. Nora Praeger comes over to Dave and leans down and smells his flannel shirt quickly. "You don't smell like you've never had a bath."

"Well," he says, cringing a little at her closeness, "I have actually. But the reason is that the oils of the skin don't make you smell that bad. It's what animals probably smelled like when they were alive."

More talk. "Well yes," Kellner says, "the principle makes sense. Negate all the falsifications of nature that civilization sneaks on you and you've got a chance."

"Speak English, come on."

"Our vulnerability to Ceph is due to the falsifications of nature provided by civilization. Don't you see, the boy's father was right. Why do you think he makes it all the way down here?" He points at Dave. "He's from the north, the rural north. That's why I told you a long time ago that before I came here, I crossed fresh tracks and lots of them." Everyone laughs. It is apparently an old boring story.

"Wait," Dave says, "what do you mean by tracks?"

"What I said. Oh, you can't have heard. I told these people here and the authorities that in rural Oregon, east of Portland by a hundred miles, I looked down in the mud and saw fresh tracks, of what seemed like some hooved animal. I wasn't dreaming." The others sit bored. One rises to get a fish patty.

"Well I saw a bird," Dave says. "Only a few years ago."

A new topic: Herb Kellner is standing now, arms out, like a fired up orator. He repeats his original thesis, that there is a strong probability that animals live in the north. The penetrating force of Kellner's voice makes Dave's mind switch to an almost dreamlike, marginal attentiveness. Swooning in a necessary self defense, it cocoons in on itself and concentrates on the repetition of the four names.

Those tracks were years after the second wave!

Meaning an animal lives in the north.

Shut up. Let me talk. Why? Because it is cold, because the conditions favored by the germ are temperate climates. Maybe Dave saw some migratory bird. Hey, tell us about it.

Huh? Dave shakes his head and expands on the sighting of the bird. Kellner pounds the table exhultantly. Yes, he says, my tracks, your bird. Two proofs against you and them. He pokes his thumb toward the Complex, which, through the window, flickers on this clear evening with a million dots of light. This boy has come to confirm to us that we're all wrong, we're all in the wrong place!

Aw Herb, my *ears*.

There he is, Kellner says, the ignorant prophet (excuse, it wasn't meant as an insult).

No sweat. (Thurston, Keene . . .)

You saw a bird. There you are, proof that what I said was more than delusion.

How do we know what he saw—

I saw what I saw.

Hey Herb, why didn't you stay in Oregon then?

I accepted the assumption that I would die without medicated food.

Or you couldn't stand the idea of mating with a cow?

You don't want to take this seriously do you?

What's the medicine? Dave asks dully.

Well, there's an antibiotic that knocks off whatever you get, when you get it.

My Dad said that medicine was the first way to get the germ. It makes the body vulnerable. All systemic medicines.

That's a matter of opinion, a soft voice from the corner says. The idea is that either the race dies because it modified its resistance by the use of medicines, or it tries to go back to establishing natural resistance. That's what your father figured was the best way, or the only available way. The government took the road of doing something about the new lack of resistance. Invent medicines which overturn what the other medicines have already done. Besides, there's no way they could have established natural resistance again. Everybody would have died in training.

Well Dave didn't.

How many other people live up there?

Three.

Other towns?

My Dad said north, some. Some in Canada too, he said.

You know who sits there with that fuzz on his upper lip and that small beginning of a beard? Kellner says. Dave strokes his modestly hairy chin. We have a result of a reduction, a massive process of selection. You ever been sick?

Nope.

How about a cold? Everybody gets that.

My Dad said I had them, but I didn't know I had them.

Lemme ask, Herb says. Let's say in winter, did your father keep you inside, make sure you were all warm and all?

No, the opposite—inside the house it was a cold as outside. He made me work in winter in shirtsleeves.

Brilliant. See? His father perpetrated the reduction, made the process of selection happen. Here's the result.

Nah, he just watched out for himself.

Maybe he's a three dimensional TV image. Eh Herbie, how about that?

Sure, he's a figment of my imagination.

Oh God I can't take any more of this.

Me either, I'm getting the hell out.

My mind's bent, bent all to hell.

When Dave looks up again out of a peculiar half sleep, he sees that the lounge is empty.

"I would like to have known your father," Kellner says. He looks off from the porch of the fourth floor hall of the building at the twinkling profile of the Complex. "Seems to have had a lot of it nailed down."

"Yeah, he worked on it a lot," Dave says, yawning.

"Wonder why he sent you here though. Here you got yourself equipped to survive anywhere, and he sends you here?"

"Getting here was supposta be what it was all about."

"Then why not five years ago?" Dave shrugs. "Know what?" Kellner says, "once you're in there you can't ever come out without croaking. Because the environment in there will soften you again, to the point where you'll lose all your resistance." He looks at the profile, his face growing contemplative and distant. "I used to live in Dubuque, Iowa y'know. Smelled like a slaughterhouse, the whole town, cause that's where they packed meats. One time there was this flood in the Mississippi? All the fish in the river swam inland because of all the grass and weeds and stuff to explore, and then the water receded, leaving half of them in these pools of evaporating water.

Never seen anything like it. Ranks of them, Carp, Dogfish, in these hot pools, gulping and dying and smelling up the place. I can't figure whether I feel like one of the fish stranded on the banks or one of the ones left in the river."

"Well, at least you're alive."

"The weather scares me," Kellner says. "Y'know, I'll bet you've come into close contact with the Ceph lots of times. Why do you think you're still alive? Why do you think any of these people here are still alive? Not luck. It's that they're the core of those tough enough to survive. It's a reduction, like I said. The worst problem here is sanitary conditions."

"I don't know—this is Ceph. Deers and skunks and stuff didn't have problems with sanitary conditions."

Kellner laughs. "Yeah, you're right. Tell you something, though. I saw a track, you saw a bird. The whole thing'll start itself over again. The only aberration, the only fluke in the whole process is that," and he nods his head toward the lights of the Complex. "There's the fluke. Poor bastards in there can never come out. Die in a month. And you know what? They're killing us too, with the medicine food. There's all kinds of food we could eat, but they say eat only what they tell us to, mostly medicated stuff, and that ruins your liver. Antibiotics give you cirrhosis, screw up all your plumbing."

Dave chuckles. Sure, the guy might be right, but it still seems to him that the Complex must be preferable to any other alternative.

"Well," he says, "tomorrow I'll go in and write you a letter tellin' you what it's like."

"Too bad, cause you got the stuff to start it over. And those others who travelled out of here? They aren't dead, not all of them anyway. And punks—how do they survive?" Kellner squints, slowly shakes his finger at the lights. "It's all wrong—what they should be doing is sending out little families or something, figure out some way to communicate, maybe even recruit punks. Anyway, see if it's possible to start up new communities. That's what they should do. Not this. Why the hell are we all jammed up together here? We should spread out. I mean hell, there would be little groups of people going around just deciding where to live. Christ, there are enough nice towns, beautiful houses." He looks at his wristwatch. "Wanna see where you're going? C'mon, it's just around the corner. The weekly report. TV propaganda from the Complex."

"Films?" Dave asks. "You mean like moving picture film?"

The paradise that tantalizes him from only a kilometer away reveals itself on the large screen in a meeting hall next to his residence unit. He sits shoulder to shoulder with the other people of his house and strangers from the block and sees films of news from inside the Complex. It is amazing. On the screen he sees real life. When the picture shifts, he follows a form with his eyes right off the edge into the black fringe of the bright moving picture, once almost falling off his seat. He is made dizzy, almost nauseous by the bright box which sweeps over reality, races into it and back out. On a verdant field of artificial grass under thousands of lamps the tryouts for the Olympics are held. Aside from the sky, which is in reality a domed ceiling, everything looks normal. The narrator briefly describes the records, expectations, rules of the discus, shot put, pole vault and different runs.

The medical report says that the expected loss outside the Complex due to hazardous weather conditions this year is one hundred thousand, barring unforseen circumstances. The audience shuffles, whispers, while off in front younger refugees come out with a hoarse, sustained boo. The moderator says that this year's outbreaks will not approach the catastrophic levels of the previous year in the Staten Island sectors. The scene shifts to a gleaming laboratory where the technicians and doctors work under rigid codes of caution on test animals, in pursuit of a cure for the Ceph. The moderator says that one recent finding dulls the hopes of the people: aside from the host transference capability of the germ, they now suspect different strains of the microvirus. What may be a cure for one may not be a cure for another, hence multiplying the problem. However, he says, those refugees on the outside have little to fear as long as their medications are kept up and as long as there is no relaxation of the standards of hygiene recommended by the authorities.

The news shifts to the food reports: Dave sees sleek ships pulling in massive catches of ocean fish. He sees huge greenhouses, conveyors carrying vegetables. The film switches in one second segments from the entrance at the harbor to the huge solar generators on the roof of the Complex to steaming laboratories underneath, all amounting to a demonstration of the processing of the foods. When this segment is over he must look away to reorient himself. Then there is an interview inside a residence unit, which looks compact but well organized, with nice looking plastic furniture and recessed lighting. The interview is with a worried wife of a man who is going on trial for some crime and is threatened with removal from the Complex. The younger bunch in front hoots and jeers, yells out different suggestions—hey, I'll take your place turkey! Hey lady trade him in on me! Once a punk always a punk!

The global report includes film from the Black Sea Complex, describing the discoveries of uses of geothermal energy, describing a case of infection which turned up inside a sealed zone in the Complex and was dealt with by automatic means whereby an entire ten thousand cubic meter sector was closed off. This proves, the moderator says, the necessity for rigid controls on cross sector travel inside the Complex system, and the senate committee on social organization adds to the Russian report that in our Complex, it is unlikely that any case spread of parasitic microencephalitis will ever emerge inside because of the systematic efficiency of our living. "The only danger," a senator says, "is that some fissure caused by a natural phenomenon like earthquake could cause a breakdown, which we believe would be checked anyway by the structural principles of our model. Blakely understood better than any man the principles of structural flexibility."

This time, although he cannot bring himself to believe it will happen, the section of wall to the left of the thick, greenish window, opens for him. A voice in a speaker directs him into a box the size of a phonebooth. The voice orders him to remove his clothes. "What?" he says. The voice repeats the order. He does so, quickly, shaking with nervousness, straining inside the tight confines of the box. The voice orders him to deposit the clothes into a kind of hamper in the wall, and then a slot above it spits out the end of a little ticket. The voice orders him to raise his arms, which he does, and then the box whirrs, and bright green bulbs of light travel up from the floor to the ceiling. Dave trembles, smelling his fear. The machine clicks off, and something rolled up in plastic comes part way out of the wall in front of him. The voice orders him to put it on. He opens the bag with trembling hands and finds that it contains a pair of green underpants and a blue smock with baggy leggings and big pockets. When he is finished dressing the voice orders him to remove the claim ticket from the slot. It is apparently for the return of his clothes.

The voice invites him out of the box, and tells him

that his footwear are on the hall floor. When he opens the door he finds a pair of blue slippers waiting for him, pointing down a hall identical to the one he came down to go to the window. The voice then tells him to reclaim his appointment papers and identification at the end of the hall. He puts on the slippers and walks on down the hall, feeling a peculiar fear at not having his bow or bike with him. They are back at his room, bequeathed to Kellner should he be admitted today. The ceiling in this hall has the little gas nipples and the sign every ten meters: Q 23 Do Not Tamper With Ceiling Gas Jets.

He emerges into a vast, low ceilinged room. Here and there small groups of people mill about, laugh, call from one group to another. "Hunter," someone says. He turns. A man sitting at a desk waves him over. "J032851. Here're your papers." He takes them, and the man gives him a little plastic card the size of the old credit cards he had seen. His name and number are pressed into it. "Use that for the machines," the man says. "Say, you ever been here before?"

"Nope."

"Well, it's your ticket to everything, the machines, anything you buy."

"Just— Like show it to people?"

"Put it in slots in machines," the man says. "You'll see."

Dave shrugs and turns back to the hall. Looking at it, he is reminded of something he once saw in a magazine: a bus station. It looks like a bus station. It might be the size of a school gymnasium, with a flecked marble floor, plastic seats here and there, some ripped a little and then repaired with slightly mismatched tape, ashtrays with black marks where cigarettes were put out. Sound reverberates in a soft rush of taps, voices, whirrs of machinery. The light is bright and shadowless, and the air is cool and dry and irritates his nostrils, as does the funny, aseptic odor rising from the smock. He looks at the slip. Q23 Office of Records, Rm. 501. He is supposed to go to an interview, he guesses, or to some kind of a registration. Off the huge room there are other narrow hallways, metal doors, some with men sitting or reading or dozing on high chairs. Guards? No one notices him. He walks slowly around the outer perimeter of the room, and passes a kind of bar. Behind it, under a wall decorated with what look like labels from old bottles sits a young man reading a newspaper. Dave approaches, clears his throat, and says, "Where's 501?"

"Huh? Across over there, down that hall. Interview?"

"Yeah, nine o'clock. Supposta live in here, I guess."

"Well, you got a few minutes to wait. Want something to drink?"

"Sure, what do you have?"

"Soft drinks. Here, a Coca Cola."

He turns in his high seat, puts a plastic glass under a spigot and pulls a handle. Dave tries it. The foam pumps his cheeks out—he has difficulty swallowing it. "What's this?"

"Coca Cola. Never had any?"

"Nope."

"Where you from, the middle ring?"

Dave repeats his story in summary, and each sentence is interrupted briefly by a "no kidding" or a "Jesus". Finally he ends up by mentioning the interview.

"Any minute now," the guy says.

"Nobody worries about the Ceph here?"

No. The man runs it down for him: the Complex is ringed with these quarantine sectors, containing offices, residence for military personnel and for service personnel, and for others who work in any capacity on the outside. He introduces himself: Bob Roberts. He lives in a little apartment down one of the halls across the huge room. He cannot leave Quarantine Sector 23 because the non quarantine sectors are full. Cross sector travel is generally restricted in the summer, unless you have a pass. He works this little bar five days a week, has two days off. On off days he spends time at the pool or in one of the many rec rooms in his sector. "You'll see them if you go down that hall over there, next to the one where the Records Office is."

"Are there ever breakouts here?"

"No—it's the air. It has a sterilizing element."

"And then that box with the lights? That kills germs too?"

"Box? What box?"

Dave explains. Bob Roberts shrugs. He has never heard of it.

"I'll be your representative for now," Mr. Carver says, shaking Dave's hand. "Now sit down, let's talk."

Dave sits, hanging his hand down by his side as if it is infected. Then he rubs it on the thigh of his smock. He repeats his story. Mr. Carver glances down at an open manila folder in which Dave recognizes a xerox of his certificate.

"Well well well," Mr. Carver says. "Let me explain how things sit—in your case we have a number of legal options which can be taken, but my advice is to opt for service."

"What's that? Ain't I just supposta come in?"

"Of course," he says, "but there are conditions under which anyone goes in. The responsibility of the governing authorities here is to assign you a suitable function. The idea is that everybody has to pull his share, as they say. Myself included. When I came here they looked at my records and decided that I was fit for a certain administrative function, so here I am," and he smiles, holding his hands out, palms up.

"Okay, so what's the service option then?"

"Well, let's see, can you read?" Dave nods. "Good, that's very good. Now, your, your history suggests that you'd qualify as a field military, and since you can read, you'd get ahead quickly in that field. Do you follow me?"

"Field militarys are the guys who spray people."

"Well, true, true, there are hazards, but it's one of the options that you are qualified for."

"What else can I do?"

"Sanitation, maintenance—"

"I'll take the maintenance."

"Well, I'll indicate that you prefer that, and we'll see. This has to go to personnel." He shuffles the papers, nods.

"Okay, where do I sleep?"

"First you have to have a medical profile, and all of that, including looking at the results, takes three days. Barring any irregularities, you'll be living here by, let's see, Tuesday."

"You mean I can't stay now? What irregularities?"

"That's not for me to decide," he says, giving Dave a sympathetic smile.

"Seems funny when I got a ticket to come in," he says, "and what's this thing they gave me?" He looks down at the front of his blue smock.

"That's standard leisure wear—see more of it on evenings."

"Do you live here?"

"Yes, only a few blocks away." He laughs. "Well, in here it would be halls. But it's pretty close by."

"Listen, if I get to be a maintenance, can I go wherever I want?"

"Sure," he says with an amiable smile.

"Like, like on the screen outside they showed a

picture of the Olympic tryouts—and once in a magazine I saw a picture of a zoo. Can I go there?"

"Oh, you misunderstand. That's up in the center. That's a different part. We've got our own zoo right here."

"How many people live in Q23?"

"Supposed to be five thousand."

"I don't understand. You mean I got to stay in this part here? Can't I ever go up to the center?"

The man laughs again with that sort of tranquil amiability which has been irritating Dave a little. "We have everything right here. Look around. Have you looked around?" When Dave says nothing, he continues, "Well you do that. Look around. Q23 is a module, like dozens of others—it's a complete society. It's done this way because they're gradually recognizing that cross sector travel left wide open is too dangerous, especially in the summer. Look, once you're in for good, you'll get the idea of the system. Your freedom to move about will increase as you continue to fulfill your function."

"Well, I guess I'll go look around then."

"Get your medical check first. 503. Two doors down."

An hour later Dave emerges from the medical checkup with a bandage on the inner crook of his left arm and the promise to himself that he will never again in his life get a medical checkup.

It seemed simple enough at the outset—the doctor, whose name was Proctor and who therefore he would not mention Breen's name to, looked in his eyes, ears, throat. Behind him a nice looking nurse fiddled with instruments on a silver tray. Then the doctor told him to take his smock off, which he did, looking at the nurse a couple of times to see if she would leave the room. She did not. Then the doctor told him to take the underpants off, and Dave stood and looked at him with suspicious irritation, but the doctor would have none of that and said come on, come on, I haven't got all day. The nurse giggled softly, fiddling over her tray, once in a while looking over her shoulder at Dave, who glared back at her, which only seemed to make her more humored. It was awful. The doctor held his testicles in his hand and told him to cough. He fiddled with them, poked around for what seemed an eternity, saying c'mon, hold still each time Dave squirmed and fidgeted. Then the doctor brusquely turned him around and told him to bend over, and Dave's brain froze with anger and he said, no. The nurse burst out laughing, and Dave said fuck you, lady, and the doctor, not humored at all by the situation, suggested that if he wanted entry into the Complex he'd better straighten himself up and stop behaving in this manner. Now do as I said, the doctor said. So Dave did it, grumbling under his breath but loud enough for both of them to hear.

Then the doctor went off to write in a pad and the nurse came over with a needle, and Dave stood there with his teeth gritted, looking at his smock hanging forlornly over the chair. What are you going to do with that? he asked, and she said she just needed a little blood and he said no, and again the doctor advised him to straighten up again, so he held his arm out and watched her poke the needle into his arm and watched the blood slowly fill the glass tube, and then he looked down the top of her uniform at the breasts squashed together there, and barely restrained the impulse to reach up and grab one. Because of his anger he barely felt the needle. Then she did something else at the tray and asked him for some urine and handed him a little plastic cup. He turned around and tried to produce some, but it was useless. If you want it, you gotta let me put my clothes back on, he said. After a brief negotiation, they allowed him to hide behind a little white sheet screen on wheels. That way it worked. The doctor asked him if he knew his number and he said yes, and the doctor said keep your ears open, because he had a memo there that indicated someone else wanted another interview with him. You can put your things back on now, he added.

Seems to me kinda stupid to make me take 'em off in the first place, he said. The doctor sighed, shook his head, muttered something about how you meet all kinds, and while his back was turned Dave held up his middle finger at him, and the nurse burst out laughing once more.

Still grinding his teeth with irritation at the memory of the medical check, he scans the large hall once again. The little groups are still there, smoking and drinking their soft drinks. Now he sees that some of them wear the same blue smock they gave to him and feels a little less out of place. He goes back to the bar and asks for another Coca Cola. "How'd it go?" Bob Roberts asks.

"Okay."

Another man standing at the bar regards him with a smirk. The bartender seems worried. "No grief, Russo. Been a long day."

Russo laughs. "Okay. Hey kid, how'd what go?"

"Medical check? Say, what do you do around here?"

The man guffaws, takes a sip. "Who'd you just talk to?"

"A guy named Carver? And some doctor?"

Russo mutters something under his breath.

"Hey," the bartender says, "c'mon, no grief."

"What'd he say?" Dave says softly. "What's the matter?"

"Nothin' kid," Russo says. "Forget it."

"What *do* you do?"

"Wait for more chicks to come in." Dave squints at him. "How many chicks you see around, kid?"

Dave looks. In the room, which now contains about thirty people, has seven. "Seven, so?"

"That's about the ratio, I figure."

"Something's wrong with your eyes, Russo," Bob Roberts says. "Ratios are fixed, you know that."

"Carver," Russo says. "I don't know that one," he says to Bob Roberts. "Is he new or something?"

"Take it easy," Roberts says.

"Stupid dipshit," Russo says.

Dave laughs. "Why do you call him that?"

"Because that's what he is, kid," Russo says louder.

Roberts is agitated. He goes down to where Russo stands and says something to him in an intense but unintelligible whisper. Russo keeps nodding as if to say okay, okay. Finally he wanders off to join one of the little groups.

"What bothers him?" Dave asks.

"Who knows?" Bob Roberts says. "Some people don't know when they're well off. He's gonna be kicked out if he doesn't watch it."

"What *does* he do?"

"Maintenance, like me."

"How many maintenance people are there? I mean, if you're maintenance, who isn't?"

"Oh, you mean management, officials, legislative types? The Q sectors are all maintenance. They call them quarantine because this is the first place you come to on your way in. After a while you're supposed to be able to travel in further, but it all depends on the bug."

"Where do the legislative personnel live?"

"Not here," Bob Roberts says, "up toward the center."

"Have you ever been to where they live?"

"I don't know—been all around though, along the

quarantine sectors and in some of the service sectors. But only in winter. It depends on the bug."

Dave explores to the limits of Q 23. He walks down hall connected to hall, dizzied by the shadowless light, and by the air which irritates his nostrils. It is a dreamlike wandering. He stops at archways opening into game rooms where the pock of pingpong games comes to him in muffled softness, where people splash in small and steamy pools and slick girls pull themselves up on the marbled walkways around the edges, stand up, adjust their scant bathing suits and dive back in. Nearby, more lie under hot lamps, their skin dark and slick with oil, the men lying close by talking softly to them and absent mindedly moving their hands over bellies and rumps. Off in the corner, a girl sits nestled between the legs of her boyfriend, who chats with her while he slowly rubs her breasts, and she clumsily twirls her bathing suit top on her finger. Dave blinks in disbelief at the picture—it is crowded, seething, and they seem to mindlessly wallow in each other with a kind of languid and tired pleasure. This excess of naked contact seems an absurd opposite to the world outside. He stumbles on, discovers another large room which is a botanical garden, steaming and green, with the heavy scent of flowers billowing out the door. In a residence section he passes open doors where he interrupts animated conversations by passing slowly by, and each time he catches a brief glimpse: they sit entwined like mating slugs, their hands slowly moving over each other. Behind them are coffee tables, pictures on walls, bottles of wine sweating on trays. Yes, this is more like it, more like what he saw in the magazines.

Anything you want is free, he discovers. In little anterooms vending machines offer soft drinks, cigarettes, kleenex, prophylactics, food wafers, various household items. All he has to do is slide his little card into the slot, and he becomes so intrigued with these machines that inside of a half hour he finds his pockets full and his hands burdened by cans of soft drink, kleenex, wafers, and has to ditch them on top of a machine. Everywhere he goes the ceiling floats only a couple of feet above his head, spaced evenly by the little nipples of gas jets.

The center of the sector is a high ceilinged circular hall with a growth of plants in the center and stores and little theaters and bars all around the perimeter. He does not know where this circular hall is in connection with the first big room he entered, and finds after further exploration that it can't be more than two minutes' walk from it, but the walk is made longer by the fact that the halls leading to it are not straight, they turn, curve, divide, even seem to rise and fall slightly.

At the opening back into the first big room he entered he runs into Russo. "Hey," he says.

"Looking around, eh kid? Roberts told me you were new."

"Yeah. Hey, what was that you were talkin' about back before? Why'd you call that guy a name?"

"Well," he says, "I walks up to a garbage can right? Am I supposta call it a rose?" Dave squints, and Russo laughs, says, "Ah I don't know. They've tightened up—useta be that I'd go over into one of the service sectors. Go see a nurse over there. Month ago I go to the gate, right? Cross sector travel is prohibited, they say. Why I say. They don't explain. Fact, they sort of treat me like shit. Like they decide not to let me in because of my appearance or something." He thinks, snorts softly. "And I'm goddam sure there isn't any fifty fifty ratio here—it's like they took all the horny good looking ones and shipped them in toward the center so some of the stupid desk jockeys could have harems."

"What do you do?"

"I'd show you if I could—I tend valves. Yeah, no kidding, tend valves, about a hundred fifty meters straight down. All I see is a million pipes, and all I do is monitor a computer screen that tells me to open this, close that. And they're getting a little tight on me cause they're afraid I'm going hostile. I might open the wrong goddam valve."

"You ever been in the center of this place?"

"Not that I know of. Hard to tell where you are, though."

He sees an official coming in his direction. Russo looks too, snorts, and then says, "see ya, kid. Beginning to smell a little rank around here."

The uniformed official comes up. "Hunter?"

"Yeah."

"We've got a page on you—come this way."

"Page? What kind of a page?"

The fact of his being led by two men into a tiny room draws attention from most of the people in the hall. They watch, whisper, talk, craning their necks in his direction, as sliding doors close them off. Then, when the room jerks, Dave says, "Watch out!" and braces himself in a corner. The two guards laugh.

"This is a elevator?" One nods. "Where we goin'?"

The guard jerks his head up. "What makes you such a big deal?" he says.

"Beats me."

The guard seems disgruntled about it. The little room sighs upward, then seems to shift into moving at a forty five degree angle pitch. All three adjust their bodies to the motion. When the elevator finally slows down and comes to a stop, the two guards look at each other with a kind of excitement in their eyes. The doors open to a carpeted hallway occupied by a guard with a pistol strapped at his waist.

"Hunter?" The two guards nod their heads at Dave. "Okay, come along. Return the elevator to 23."

He is not sure how to identify the hall he is led to. It seems to be a waiting room of some sort, with nice furniture arranged around low tables with magazines spread out, and potted plants here and there. The ceiling emits soft music. When he sees a uniformed nurse behind a window, he figures it is another doctor's office complex. An old man in a white smock approaches. "Hunter?" he says. Dave nods. "Well, we'd like very much to talk with you."

The man has a strange, sort of grandfatherly look, with a white goatee and a halo of graying hair. Dave cannot remember seeing anyone older.

"Whatcha wanna know?"

"Come this way."

His office is a strange combination of luxury and advanced science. One wall is loaded with consoles, flashing buttons, TV screens. The rest of the office is plush and deeply colorful. The desk is a huge slab of some deep red wood covered with a thick layer of amber resin holding in it a suspension of sea shells, coins, ancient trinkets. Dave's concentration is magnetized by it, by the rich, hypnotic depth of the coating of resin. He is brought out by the nameplate on the desk—D. S. Keene, Md. He decides to wait before mentioning Breen's name.

Keene turns in his chair, thinking, and then says, "Well, tell me about life upstate." Now Dave notices that Keene has a large brown mole on the upper lid of one of his eyes, so that each time he blinks, the spherical mole jerks down and up. It is positioned on the rim where it interrupts the line of eyelashes, and looks so irritating that Dave looks away as he speaks.

His mind becomes fogged in the droning repetition of the story, which he feels he has told a thousand times—the fires, deaths, disposals, stench, the gradual accumulation of rules imposed by his father, buffer zones of safety, means of maintaining the body's purity and natural strength, the whole education amounting to a singleminded, encyclopedic organization of memory itself, all around that center, the body, and its permanent adversary, the bug. Each time he stops to wait for the old man's response, looking again at that mole flicking with each blink, there is a short silence, then, "well, go on, go on—" and he shrugs and continues, feeling he has already exhausted the subject.

In the idle search for something else to say, he finds that he is slowly reinterpreting his father's life work, away from the elaborate but practical list of rules toward something else: he begins talking about the proper organization of his life as if it were a philosophy or a religion rather than a practical science: "—like that stuff about the simple stuff you gotta eat and the stuff about skin—when you break the rules you kinda ruin the sorta completeness, the, uh, the *what*chacallit, like, the safe aloneness of—"

"What? You mean autonomy?"

"What's 'at mean?"

"The—," and he turns, his chair making a long spring stretching screech. "Let's find a simple word." He pokes buttons on a little console behind him and reads, "independence."

"Yeah. Hey, what is that thing?"

"Oh, a dictionary."

"Independence," Dave says. "That's it. Once you ruin that you're done for. It isn't just bein' six feet away either. It's more something else."

"I'm not sure I completely understand."

"That wholeness is like an—an attitude, like bein' happy or sad or somethin'. See, it's like the germ sorta knows what body's ready. It's the body that ain't sorta autonomous?"

The doctor chuckles. "That's very interesting."

"Like a state of mind sorta. Like it makes your—your soul ready for the bug." He sits back, staring at the desk. He never thought of that. Belief. You kept from getting the bug by belief. Or else how the hell could he ever have survived? There couldn't be any other explanation. He realizes that his father's elaborate defense system was only half of it, that without the safety of the little potent defensive globe of belief in your own wholeness, you might as well give up. For that matter, since he came here his transgressions were not only physical, they were philosophical, and for all practical purposes he is already maggot food.

"—like when you got it, when there isn't any hole in it, then you're complete." He wants to talk on, since talking is a form of inventing out of the raw, half conscious part of his mind. "Like with the bow and arrow—when you got it, you can hit an apple at fifty feet, cause you're all whole, see? And when you don't have it, your aim is all screwed up?"

"Well," Keene says, "we haven't ruled out biological determinism, but that's only because we haven't ruled out anything."

"What's that?"

"Just what you're saying. If that was true, how come everybody got the bug?"

"Because you can't have only one and make it." The doctor stares at him. "Cause you gotta do both—the rules and the other, the stuff about whatchacallit." He stares at the flicking mole. "My father got it cause his—" He looks at the desk. "Cause his soul was out of whack."

"Ah, a malfunctioning soul," Keene says. "Very interesting."

"You think it's funny?"

"No. I'm about willing to think anything now." He pauses, looking distracted. "So, his soul misfired eh? A leak in his soul?"

"Yeah, whatever."

"My colleagues'll be very interested to hear this. Y'know, we've been chasing this for many years, millions of test animals, millions of hours of work, and I confess that I have never heard this one before." The mole droops as he stares down at his desk. "Well, let's be reasonable. I think it's simple—there are people who apparently are immune to the Encephalitis, and you're one of them."

"Nobody's immune."

"Well," he says, "let's say nearly immune, or immune under generally sanitary conditions. It's something we don't know about blood, or maybe about cellular defense or something. That's about all there is to it."

"I don't believe it."

"Of course not. You wouldn't. What good would all your—your whatchacallit be?" he says, smiling.

Dave looks around the office once more. "Hey, where's the President of the United States live?" Keene squints at him. "I was just wonderin'."

"Seaside part of the slope. This is the west side. Legislature part faces the ocean. This is mostly medical and cultural. Okay, let me hear about disposal, and all you know about all the other whole souls who live up there."

Now he talks around the ragged edges of his earlier story. As he is part way through describing the disposal of bodies according to his father's instructions, one of the larger console screens bleeds from a washed out greenish grey into a color picture of some large hall filled with people wearing grey smocks. The picture is strange because of its perspective—people walking slowly across the screen do so in a curve which alters the height of their bodies as they pass.

"What's the matter?"

"I was looking at the TV," Dave says. Keene turns

and looks too. "Funny picture."

"Fish eye lens," Keene says. "Something's wrong."

"What's it a picture of?"

"Our little holding tank for ED's. That's emotionally disturbed people. Insane asylum, you'd call it." He squints into the picture. "What the hell—" and presses a button under the screen. "What's the monitor want?"

"Back of the hall," a woman's voice says. Keene punches another console button repeatedly, which brings the back of the picture up in jerks. He homes in on a man lying on his back on the floor, staring at the ceiling with a kind of catatonic objectivity. Dave's face twists slowly into a wince of recognition. The man is crazy, and the rest of the people shuffling around pay no attention to him. They, too, wander in a sleepy lack of comprehension, their eyes unfocused. The funny, warped perspective of the picture makes it all the more horrible and fascinating.

Keene punches something out on a computer console—the machine clicks rapidly and flashes white writing on a black screen. "Okay," he says into a little desk box, "remove the patient and administer what's indicated on his chart." He seems angry about something. "And next time, exercise the simple ingenuity of figuring this out for yourself, okay?" He shakes his head and looks back at the screen. Two men in white pass through the milling people and pick the man up by the armpits and feet and carry him out of the picture. "These people are on an exercise walk," Keene says. "That's our disease. That and liver damage."

"Liver damage is bad," Dave says. "People I stayed with on the outside say the medicine food does it."

"True." The doctor punches the console picture back to its broader perspective.

"Lotta people go nuts here?"

"Yes. It's the—the meaning of being here. The sense of—"

"Locked up," Dave says. "Is there a percentage?"

Keene looks at him again, the mole bobbing. "That's classified."

"Must be a lot then, huh?"

"For someone who comes from nowhere, you're remarkably perceptive."

Dave waits a second, figuring that he should now mention Breen's other message. He looks once more at the people shuffling around in the picture, and says, "Mr. Breen said he wants to discuss something else with you."

The doctor's face changes slowly, so that the recognition of what Dave has said seems to creep into it from the side. Then the mole bobs quickly, three times. "Okay," he says, "we'll get to that later. Disposal. Oh, wait," and he punches out numbers on a little box on his desk. A man's voice says, "Yeah?"

"Keene. Look, I want to discuss 7215—on the console? They just took him out."

The man on the other phone laughs. "What for?"

"No, no, I've got an idea. Come by."

When he signs off, he asks again about disposal and decomposition. While Dave talks on, Keene writes on a pad, and whenever Dave pauses, Keene says "go on," in that same voice he used before, but his face is now lined with agitation, and the mole flicks frequently. Dave's description of burials, Charlie's grappling hook trick for dragging bodies attached to long ropes, is finally interrupted by the arrival of a younger doctor wearing a smock like Keene's.

"Hold it," Keene says. "7215, I want to try something—could we talk about this now?" He holds the pad up in front of the other doctor's face. "I was thinking of taking him off everything and doing our megavitamin diet thing."

The other doctor's face turns color and he looks quickly at Dave with an excited smirk. Keene turns to Dave. "Would you mind holding off for now—why not come with us for lunch, and we can continue later."

As it works out, they usher Dave out of the office and through the large reception room to a long hall, all the way talking about 7215. The doorway they push him through opens out to a mammoth arcade with a high, vaulted ceiling, at least twenty meters high, and at ground level there are gardens, colorfully dressed people, a little quick tramway running through the center, and thousands of sounds, but all reduced into a strange, auditory velvet by the plush acoustics of the place. It is so amazing to him that he barely registers the voice of Keene behind him, whispering harshly to the other man, who is tryin to hold back his laughter: "I blew it! I blew it *royally*! When they hear those tapes—God, he said it and I didn't react right!"

"Aw shit, c'mon, don't worry—I'll cover somehow. Main thing's we gotta figure out how the fuck a megavitamin diet is anything new. Coulda come up with something better than that," and the man continues laughing.

"This is bad," Keene says. The other doctor turns and looks at Dave.

"So, you're the immune one, eh?"

"Huh? No."

"The one from upstate. Anyway, you're only the fourth one I've seen. Three punks and a cracker," and he laughs again until the laughter degenerates into a funny series of snorts, like someone trying to imitate a pig. "Sorry," he says.

For some reason Dave seems to draw everyone's attention as they pass the colorful, mindfogging confusion of the ubiquitous richness of objects and foliage, of interesting, warmly lit nooks where groups of people sit drinking and talking. Keene nods and smiles apologetically at those who screw their faces up at Dave. Finally he realizes that it is the blue smock that draws their attention. "It's the uniform," Keene says, "standard maintenance uniform. People don't come up here."

"Ever?" Keene shrugs as he walks, as if to say, well, maybe not ever.

Dave looks around again. The people here seem dressed more elegantly, as if they had walked out of the pages of old magazines. The women all look healthy and attractive and sophisticated, and Dave wonders if maybe Russo was right about quotas. Here and there he sees children, and unlike any he has seen outside, they are neatly dressed and groomed, like dolls.

"Maxim's," Keene says. "We can talk there."

Maxim's is an eating place, off one side of the arcade and down a long flight of plushly carpeted steps. They walk past a number of darkened alcoves, and Keene peeks in one and says, "Okay, here we are."

They sit around a table inside a peculiar chamber with a bright bubble of glass on one side, and as Dave sits, he realizes it is a window—outside he sees the receding panorama of the New Jersey side of the subordinate population, the buildings, the lowhanging smoke, the distant orange glitter of windows, all fading into a washed out grey on the horizon. Closer, he sees the grid of urban streets and simple squares of building rooftops. Something seems to capture Keene's attention off on one side. "Hey, what's that?" he says. Off to the south a small square of buildings seems to sit in a low blanket of whiter smoke while above, tiny dots fuzzed at the edges move across the geometric surfaces rising from the smoke. Occasionally they glint dully as they move across the orange, smoke filtered sunlight.

"Copters," the other man says. "Outbreak?"

"Where would that be?" Dave asks.

"Way down—Elizabeth, thereabouts."

"At least there's no wind," Keene says.

"Okay," Keene's friend says, turning away from the window, "what's this about Breen wanting to talk about something else?"

"Just what I said."

"What else did he tell you?"

"I—well," and he looks out again at the square of buildings to the south, remembering Breen's warning to keep his mouth shut. "That's all he said."

"You're a bad liar kid. It's written all over your face. What did our doped up, eighty proof friend tell you?"

"Nothin' really."

"We gotta order," Keene says. "I'll punch up three regulars," and he turns to a little square of buttons on the wall.

"See this?" the other says, opening a leather case he draws from his pocket. It is a little pistol. "This is a trank gun—if you want to play coy I'll just zap you and you'll end up in a ward in a plastic bubble, and there'll be a sign on it saying Caution: suspicion of latent infection, and you'll be all alone."

"Take it easy," Keene says.

"Are you Thurston or McPherson?" Dave asks, and the man laughs again, but this time the laughter is too loud.

"Thurston," he finally says.

Dave looks once more at the little gun and tries to reconstruct for them his meeting with Breen. As he talks, Thurston periodically laughs, ending with that peculiar snorting, and Keene, his eye mole flicking, holds his own head and shakes it slowly. When Dave exhausts the story, Keene sighs and says, "My God, we've got to do something. He's gone off the deep end."

"Yes, our inebriated friend has committed an indiscretion."

"Hey," Dave says, "why couldn't we just talk in your office?"

"Everything's taped," Keene says. "A monitor system."

"Well, what should I do?"

Thurston thinks, then says, "Tell him only one thing. The franchise is terminated."

"The franchise is terminated. But where will you get your junk?"

"See how innocent that question was?" Thurston says to Keene. "Doesn't it just blow your wires the way he makes the word 'junk' sound? How'd you ever survive kid?"

Dave shrugs.

"I have never in my life heard the word 'junk' sound so phenomenally *innocent*. Doctor, butcher, junkman, milkman," he muses. "Amazing. It blows all my wires."

"Hey," Dave says, looking back out toward the square of buildings with the whiter smoke on the streets, "what about that? Is that really a breakout? Outbreak, I mean?"

Thurston squints. "Looks like it," he says. "Poor dumb fuckers."

"Shh," Keene says.

"Maybe it isn't," Thurston goes on. "Maybe it's just a minor fire that happens to burn in a perfect square." He looks, squinting thoughtfully. Then he reaches into his pocket and takes out a little plastic container of pills and quickly pops one into his mouth and swallows it with some difficulty. Keene sees him do this and glares at him.

"Don't you think that—"

"Don't worry about me," Thurston says. "I can take care of myself."

They look south. The tiny specks of hovering helicopters flash dully in the orange sunlight. As they watch, a woman dressed in a kind of shortened gown comes by with a tray with their food on it, beans, potatoes, fruit, and something Dave suspects is meat. She leans way over as she sets it out on the table, revealing opulent flesh inside the lowcut neckline, reminding Dave of Barbara. Thurston puts his hand on her waist and asks for a bottle of the house wine. Keene seems agitated about something.

" 's this meat?" Dave asks.

"Soy," Keene says. "It's so close that you'd never know—might be our most significant achievement."

"I would like to make our waitress one of *my* most significant achievements," Thurston says. Keene is squinting toward the south, watching the specks of helicopters sweep across the faces of the buildings. After the wine arrives, they eat in silence, watching the distant activity. Dave stops chewing and thinks.

"Do they gas the people?"

Thurston, who was bringing a piece of the fake meat to his mouth, stops and looks at it, his face showing a sudden change in his appetite, and a strangely inconsistent humor. "Absolutely," he says. "Of course. And then they burn the corpses with flame throwers so they just sizzle and splutter like bacon—"

"Shh," Keene says. "Stop it. Now you're getting—"

"Sizzle and splutter," Thurston says, putting his fork down, "and my oh my do they smell. Burning flesh is an interesting smell."

Dave nods, chewing. Thurston nods brightly, and Keene puts his fork down and flaps his hands once into the air.

"Smatter?" Dave asks. Keene quickly whispers

something to Thurston. "Oh, sorry," Dave says. "I didn't mean to—I mean, I useta eat all the time with that smell around. Rot, too."

Thurston pushes his plate away and looks out the bubble window. "Look there," he says. Now the square of buildings way off has enlarged into a rectangle. "Two sectors," Thurston says. His voice has changed to a strange slur. "My oh my how the population declines. Out there and in here. Slower in here 'course, since we got all the medical—"

"Shh!" Keene says. Then he looks at Dave and waves his hand as if to say pay no attention to him.

"—all medical knowledge, sure," Thurston says. "But goddam, whatcha know? Li'l Ceph here, li'l Ceph there. Can you imagine? Must be endemic to the race, must be endemic—"

He has quieted down now, and Keene sits with his face held in a kind of dull embarrassment.

"I'm sorry," Thurston says. "I am a trifle overwrought."

Dave continues chewing, trying to register the information. Ceph in here? "Hey, did he say the bug was here?"

Keene doesn't answer. Thurston has the presence of mind to shift in his chair and snort. "It'll be out in a couple weeks anyway," he says softly. "What the hell. Sure it's in here. Always been."

"How many people know?" Dave asks.

"Plenty," Keene says. "It isn't that much of a secret."

"How many people got the bug in here?"

"That is classified," Thurston says, regaining his composure. "Even if it wasn't I wouldn't tell you. Kid, this has been a bad enough day without you even."

"Well I was just transferring a message."

"Yeah, sure. Well, what the hell, we control it in

here, eh?" He looks at Keene, who still stares dully at the table.

"Yeah," he finally says.

When it comes time for Dave to leave, Keene sends Thurston off, whispering to him first, and then accompanies Dave to the elevator. "Listen, don't think we're crooks," he says. "That other business is more a distracting pain in the neck than anything else."

"Yeah. The franchise is terminated, right?"

"Right—we'll contact you again. This survival business has always interested me. Some day I'm going to recommend training people for it."

"That is if you don't knock off the Ceph."

Keene shakes his head. "That doesn't seem likely. Look, about Dr. Thurston's little, well, implication there, forget it. Don't mention it. If it comes out, and it will, let the PR people handle it. Our cases are all singular and isolated anyway—we never have outbreaks."

"Look, if I'm goin' back out, what are the chances that the break we saw from the window'll—"

"No. Miles south. No problem. Your residence sector is in the direct administrative subordinate population. Fewer people. No problem. Look, don't think badly of Thurston either. He's a fine doctor and he's been working on this for many years. Everybody's discouraged, that's the problem. This disease—it does things to people."

"Yeah, I know."

"And keep your mouth shut about everything we said. Everything. Even if you do talk, we'll deny it anyway, but we can't stand any more suspicion after this last year or so. We've got a tough legislature now, and they don't mess with the laws. And they're tightening everything up because the bug's on the increase in here. Nobody knows why, but it's on the increase, modifying itself every time we try something new. You wouldn't believe how adaptable the thing is."

Kellner the fist shaker: "You see? You see what he's telling us? He's saying that inside there, you still end up a refugee. If it hadn't been for the business about living without medicine, then he'd never have gone up to the center!"

"No Herb, in summer they restrict travel. Everybody knows that."

"Since when do they call them quarantine sectors? Thought it was service, military, etcetera. What the hell is the new name?"

"It's not a new name. Quarantine has always been a subtitle for all fringe sectors."

"They had this box with lights in it," Dave says. "They sweep up, green like."

"Yeah, yeah, we knew that—it's a kind of ray. Kills everything. Air does too."

Dave sits back, exhausted, still unable to completely absorb the information about the bug. Charlie would have said we should have known. Dave's reaction is a kind of dull acceptance of the information, almost as if it is no surprise at all, yet he knows it is the overload of experience he has accumulated in a single day which keeps him from thinking anything about it. Of course, if the bug is everywhere, superior in its efficiency, undeniable in its universality, then why shouldn't it be in there too? The only difference in there is perfect sanitary conditions.

He has had the information waiting on the tip of his tongue ever since he returned hours ago, but has decided to honor Keene's directive to keep his mouth shut. What would be the point in telling them anyway? They'd never believe it. Kellner might say it's a ruse to keep plaintiffs out, another trick to deny them their rights.

The talk goes on: "It's *summer* Herb, and besides, how do you know the guy is telling the truth?"

"You know what it is?" Herb says, "it's simple: it's another system of concentric circles of varying degrees of legitimacy. Who ever said there was complete freedom on the inside? Oh ho *ho*," he says, "I see it clear as day. Up in the center, those are the only people anywhere who get what they want."

"It's real pretty up there," Dave says, "they got—"

"Aw come on Herbie, you're fulla crap."

"Ask the scout here, he just told us."

"Yeah, but he also said in Q23 there are pools, stores, the whole works. What's the problem?"

"Cheap opiates for the servant class," he says. "Here's another one. What is the ratio of service and maintenance personnel to the rest? Or, in the old days, how many servants did the rich man have?"

"Herb, the kid's only been there *once*. What do you want? Besides, if everything's free, what the hell difference does it make?"

"Lots. The whole thing's fishy."

"Well, I'll tell you the rest when I go back."

"*If* you go back. We heard helicopters. Couple sectors over—and a case came up only a kilometer and a half away."

"Well, it won't happen here."

He has a dream: he breaks into a house in mid winter. The snow is over a foot deep and glitters in the sun. The thin layer of it on the porch squeaks as he walks on it. The door opens and he goes into a clean kitchen. In the living room a crack in the front door has permitted the formation of a delicate little snowdrift that arcs in front of the television set. There are no corpses, no evidence of death, violence or agony. He stands at the window looking out over the perfect, undisturbed blanket of snow that covers everything, knowing that in spring when it melts the corpses will poke up through and continue to rot in the sun. All is inert, all life is interrupted. He stands at the window and looks at the perfect, seamless and desolate clarity of the square of blinding white. Behind him there is absolute silence. He knows that standing there, his heart beating, his blood moving on its way through his veins, the fog of his breath coming up against his face, he knows how absolutely without meaning everything is. The word bleak comes to mind. Bleak. Like the call of some animal made with unconscious compulsion. Bleak, bleak. He is almost comfortable knowing this. Therefore there is nothing to worry about. Since existence is a dream which blinds all reason, there is comfort in realizing the absolute, desolate triviality of breath itself. Poor Charlie, blinded by the order of his own experience, can never, in all his collected wisdom, accept this simple and universal truth: it is all a flash, everything that exists is a meaningless flash in a span of time and a space of velvet nothingness that is not measurable. In the dream he lifts a blue vase and hurls it through the television screen, listens thoughtfully to the pop, and chuckles and walks out, making sure not to disturb the beautiful and glittering little snowdrift, which, now delicately perforated with little shards from the broken screen, sweeps in front of the TV set.

The air he wakes up in is ironically hot, moist, virulent with the possibility of infection.

"Of course," he says softly into the grease caked fabric of his bag, which he had placed on the bed. It is all so mindlessly simple: near New Florence he did break into that house and did, at eleven or twelve, make that recognition without knowing he made it. You just open yourself up, sort of in a swoon, to the comfortable blackness which seems almost like a mother, like a protector who comforts you and easily convinces you that the flash and all that is spun off the flash means nothing. You can't be whole without that recognition.

He waits out the days. The people at his place become increasingly sullen, moody, and when they talk, arguments break out easily. Hanging on to an almost sleepy objectivity, he chooses not to mediate the arguments by telling them about Thurston's and Keene's secret. That might be too much for them. Already the Ceph has an awful lock on their spirits, and when they become exasperated with their own endless speculation, they can always go to the window and gaze out at the symbol of their hope. Telling them would be like accusing their own god of some profound sin. And in the distance, on Monday, he hears the flapflapflopfloptuptuptup of a helicopter turning in the sky. If it happens here, he thinks, he will miss it, will be strolling in hallways in the Complex, will be leaving his door open in case anyone passing by might want to come in and talk. He spends most of his time extending on his experience inside, daydreaming with the vast arcade up in the center as a setting. He touches his skin, which is slick with a mixture of sweat and oil, thinking, even the air will be dry, crisp, and he will be as dry and cool as a sheet of paper, while out here, on into September and the fall, Kellner and the others will continue to walk hunched under the immense, threatening shadow of the bug.

He chooses Monday afternoon as an appropriate time to carry out his last task before going back to his daydreams, which are a preface to returning to the Complex. Breen—he prepares himself by going over that sentence once again: the franchise is terminated. It seems simple enough.

The guard at the sector fence stops him this time. "I'm goin' to see Mr. Breen—the, uh, hydroponics guy."

The guard makes a phonecall from his little glass booth before letting him pass. "Before seven," he says, "or you'll be picked up."

"Why the blocked fence? They closing them up?"

The guard holds his shoulders up in a sustained shrug, and Dave experiences that strange feeling of insecurity as he passes the fence.

He finds Breen packing. In the luxurious office which resembles a museum, open suitcases and boxes are spread around the floor. Breen waves him to a chair as he digs in one of the bottom drawers of his desk. "Well well well," he says, "It's my young courier. Drink?"

"No thanks."

Breen flops into his chair and wipes his forehead with a handkerchief. "Any messages from my friends?"

"Uh, they said, 'the franchise is terminated'."

Breen laughs himself into a coughing fit, and then slowly regains control, smiling with a sort of good-humored concentration on his own breath. "The—the franchise is terminated? Fantastic! Leave it to them to do it in four words."

"Well, I just—"

"No, no, please, let me bring you up to date." He thinks, tapping his temple. "Oh by the way, Barb's here—running an errand right now, but she'll be back in a wink. Anyway," and he sighs and relaxes back in his chair, acting busy and flustered. "Anyway, let's see. First, I knew it was terminated right after I sent you, that is, when I sobered up briefly. Then I became my old self again and tried to turn state's evidence so I could bargain my way in? You know, bust this evil trafficing for two entries? All that? Well, they didn't even want to listen. The cop on the phone said inquiries of that sort are indefinitely suspended—in other words, something's gone wrong in there. Dope's of no concern to them. Do you suppose our funny little death bug is chasing them around their pools and bars and esplenades?"

"What's an esplenade?"

"Every summer they become so incommunicative, so *petulant*, my friend. To what degree does interior infection concern them? I mean cases, yes—we in the administrative wing are privy to that information on occasion. You know, it slips in on a leaf of lettuce, inside a tomato. Their atmosphere keeps it from getting anywhere, but last week they went so far as to announce on TV the discovery of new strains of the bacteria—now PR stuff is always distilled way back, so as not to frighten the population. And this *weather*, this incredible *weather*—"

The door behind Dave's chair opens, and Barbara walks in, wearing her trenchcoat, probably with the .38 in the pocket. "Oh Dave," she says. "Stephen's told me all about—"

"Yeah," he says. Seeing her face brings it all back to him, and he feels that flash of familiar heat run through him, a kind of ticklish electricity.

"Well, how are you?" she says.

"Okay." She seems excited about something, as if Dave's presence is no more than a nice distraction.

"If we're going to do it," she says to Breen, "we've gotta do it soon. They're closing fences all over. Elizabeth's shut down. They're waiting it out."

"You mean an outbreak?" Dave asks.

"That's the way it goes in the summer," she says.

"So," Breen says, "it's off to the races then. Too bad it isn't spring or fall. In summer even administrators don't have any rights. Okay, you two talk, have a drink. I'm going to go get our guide." He disappears through a doorway behind his desk.

Left alone, they talk. She inquires first about the

inside, and he describes what he saw, ending with the arcade—"it's real pretty up there. They got this big hall with all these gardens and stuff, and stuff that tastes just like meat, and little windows where you can look out," and he finishes by asking what she and Breen are up to.

They are going south, to the hydroponics project. Breen cultivates a special dream of escaping death, either by the bug or by a Complex courier with a pistol. He believes that one way or the other they'll die if they stay. The bug will soon have a field day, he says. Back in the old days when they had a string of cool summers was one thing, but this is the third year of near hundred degree heat waves, and he thinks this summer the jig is up for a good part of the population.

He will establish a little empire down there, become a force to contend with, make food an item of tough bargaining—it should be easy—he has an army of restored punks sixty strong now, and the simple fact of their existence is what will establish the success of the future of the empire. The Complex people and the population rings have been killing them off for years without considering the simplest fact: they continue to live, like Dave, without medicated food. Breen knows his years are numbered, but regards them all as his children, and sees a future for them. They will run the land as far as they can range, extract goods from miners in trade for cocaine or food. He believes that these punks who have been the population's greatest pest for years are the race's hope after all. All they need is a little organization.

"—he keeps talking about America," Barbara says in a voice raised only a step above an excited, conspiratorial whisper, "that the people who first came here were like punks in a way. Anyway, I'm going with him."

"What about the bug?"

She snorts, looks toward the window where part of the grey concrete of the Complex blocks the view of the sky. "*I* won't get it," she says, "I'm just not the type."

"But how do you expect to—"

"No. The truth is I *won't* get it. I don't know how to explain. I think it's something you know."

He is amazed at her. She, in her own way, coming from her own experience, has discovered the secret. "I guess I know what you mean," he says.

"We're hijacking a government jeep, a capital offense, but Stephen's through worrying about that. There are breakouts all over, as usual, and we're gonna bust out. Neat, huh?"

"You'll never make it."

Breen returns by the same door accompanied by a tall man in a military uniform. "Here's our ticket," Breen says, pointing at him. Dave studies the face and uniform. The man is into his thirties probably, with eyes like blue ice and a smirk that clearly suggests punk.

"We stole the uniform," Breen says, "makes him look really legit, don't you think?"

"Sure." The man says nothing. He stands by the doorway as Breen continues to talk about him as if he isn't there. "I've restored him to a useful individual after fifteen years of rampaging on the fringes of civilization. I had to convince him not to kill people as a method of socializing."

The man laughs harshly and smiles. "We found him cutting holes in our greenhouses and decided to rehabilitate him instead of putting a hole in his head and presto change-o, look here, general in Breen's army of junk smuggling mercenaries. You know," and suddenly Breen's eyes become misty, and he frowns in deep thought. "You know, when people first came here England thought they were all crazy, but then after a while, they realized that these hardy, diligent folks were a new civilization, finally greater than their own."

"See?" Barbara whispers.

"And here we are, our little army, our healthy and fertile women, our bright future—"

"We'll breed like crazy," the reformed punk says.

"I knew I wouldn't have to tell you to do that. See, ingenuity."

"Yes sir," the punk says. Barbara laughs.

"Come with us, son," Breen says.

"Can't. Goin' back in tomorrow."

"Too bad. From what Barb's told me, you'd make a perfect general. Can you take a message to Keene?"

"Sure, why not?"

"Mine's two words. Tell him to fuck off. If he wants coke, and later even food, then he'll have to get word to us, and we'll consider it. I'll be in a forty room mansion with my Cutty, my young wife here, and my trusty men."

"Sounds great."

Further talk is dropped. Breen checks lists, gives instructions to his punk general. Before Dave leaves, Barbara stops him. "Listen, it'd be fun. It's kind of a revolt, and Stephen is a genius at organizing things." She pauses, looking at him. "I may be his wife as he says, but there's plenty to go around if you—"

"Well, I would, but I gotta go in. It's kinda—well, I just guess I'm goin' in."

"Sure," she says. "Guess I would too if I could."

"And what about him? How's he expect to survive?"

"All he said was just wait and see. He had this funny look on his face too, like he dared me not to believe him."

Breen too, he thinks. The least likely of all people to chuck the Complex as a dream and look for something new. "What's getting into everybody?" he asks. Barbara laughs, nodding.

"The weather, that's all. Just the weather."

He returns to his quarters quickly, walking in a kind of confusion of energy, as if he, too, should do something different from the program he is bound to follow. And the feeling of restlessness is heightened when he enters the downstairs lounge: there they are talking on, babbling out the same arguments, the same speculations, all eyes but Kellner's crossed with that shadow of fear, that recognition of the awesome possibilities of clouds of invisible virulence wafting their way.

When Kellner sees Dave he stops, squints at him. "Hey," he says, "you heard anything else?"

"Well," and he looks from person to person, considering whether he should say anything. "Well, I heard that they were closing fences all over, and that there was a big break down in Elizabeth." It makes no impression on them. "And then I heard that the people think this is the biggest year of all."

"Who told you that?"

"Some people I know." For them, the lack of a name for that source of information makes it idle hearsay. "And then when I was inside, they sorta said that they had a lot inside too." He flushes, realizing what he has said.

"Ah *ha*!" Kellner shouts. "Listen to *that*!"

The guy who usually sat in the shadows in the corner and was always so soft spoken and reasonable rises and walks slowly toward Dave, his face suddenly twisted with hatred and disbelief. "You goddam punk," he says, "just because you were in there you think you can walk all over us with that bullshit."

"Hey, I'm just tellin' you what—"

"Why don't you just get the hell out of here? We

got enough trouble without you going out and coming back with this stuff." Now he is on the edge of attack, and Dave backs up toward the door. Kellner comes over and stands between them.

"Come on," he says to the guy, "relax. Let's be reasonable about this. Take it easy."

"Just because he went inside," the guy says. "High and mighty punk. Get out of here. Leave us the hell alone."

"Okay," Dave says softly. "I mean I was just—"

"Shut up. Leave us alone."

He shrugs and leaves them to speculate on their new information.

Tuesday. The rancid warmth of the morning air he passes through makes him sweat, even though he rides his bike fast enough to create a wind against his skin. Kellner told him not to bother to leave the bike this time because the faster he got to the fence the better. The premonition was correct: across the center of one of the little concentrations of buildings is a stretched out roll of barbed wire. Soldiers patrol it. He coasts along the billowing wire and overtakes a soldier. "I wanna get through," he says. "Supposta go in today. Got an appointment?"

"Cross sector travel is prohibited until the weather gets better. Nobody goes anywhere."

"I got a ticket, a good one."

"Sorry, nobody goes anywhere."

He returns to his residence, a little shamefaced at again having to retract the multitude of goodbyes and good lucks from a half hour before. Rotten break! they say. Well, he says, what the hell, next week then.

Next week will not come as any of them expect it. Next week will not come at all for one eleven year old boy later found to be named Roy Morgan. It happens four blocks from Dave's residence. He is told by a yelled message from the street, and grabs his bow and runs down. Oh yes, see this, he thinks. Here it is, the beginning of the end. The people have established a large circle around poor Roy, and mutter in shock and confusion about the horrifying implications of what they see dead center in their circle. He is staggering on the macadam, looking around as if surprised at people's odd reaction to him. His face is hot and flushed, and his eyes are running. From thirty meters Dave can see the streaks on his face. He is mumbling softly, looking around, gesturing as if he wants to speak. He takes another step, falls down on his side. Suddenly he vomits, and what appears to be a gallon of yellowish liquid spews from his mouth in an efficient flow and splatters onto the street. Then he sits up, his hands in his lap, strings of vomit hanging from his chin. His shoulders shake with hopeless laughter.

From the direction of the Complex he hears the flapflapflapflopflupfluptuptuptup of the helicopter, which soars low in the sky above them. The voice in the loudspeaker says, evacuate the area, go back to your homes, do not attempt to leave your sector! The speaker spurts, makes a shattering splutter of static, then repeats the order. The people begin to increase the size of their circle, some of them retreating into the alleys between the buildings, some running away. There are still thirty or forty people present when the copter descends, creating a deafening clatter, and Dave sees it happen, sees the stupidity which makes it barely possible that anyone could survive here very long. He must run once he sees the process begin. Now from a hundred yards away he watches the copter come down on the dying boy, readying its equipment of extermination, and the idiots watching forget that the propeller creates a little wind outward from the source, the boy. He can see by the dust that the wind carries the germs billowing outward, close to the ground, in gentle reverse circular motion like a wheel moving in a direction opposite from its spin, and the people permit that gentle wind to engulf them, to ruffle their hair, pass them, and continue, slower, into the open windows and alleys. By the time the copter is on the boy Dave is further away, and is just able to see that the method is first a white gas and then a flame throwing device which sets the body burning vigorously.

"I could have told them it was stupid," Dave says. Everyone is glum, sitting with their chins on their fists gazing around. One of the girls has been crying. "You could see it," he says, "you could see the air, the dust—it went right to them. I can't understand it."

"Why our sector? Why us?"

"Why not?" Kellner says softly. "Every year it's some sector or other. Had to happen sooner or later." He seems almost happy about it, as if it is more important that one of his suspicions has been confirmed. Dave sits in a warm heap, his mind a combination of strange excitement and almost bored hopelessness. That confusion of secret wishes, to get in quick or to escape like that crazy old Breen, seem such direct contradictions that he feels immobilized.

"Well," Kellner says, "in a week we'll know."

"No," Dave says, "tomorrow or later today we'll know if there's any reason to wait a week." They all look at him. "It means that there are two ways for this to happen: either he's one isolated case, and he infects others who get sick seven days from now, or he is the first evidence of a sort of blanket infection. If there aren't any cases today or tomorrow, then there isn't anything to worry about for a week."

"My God the kid's right," Kellner says. "There could be thousands tomorrow."

Fifty-six is the word of mouth number so far. He

does not know how they can be so sure. It is eleven o'clock in the morning, hours after Dave has risen from the comfort of his bag. His mind ticks off the mathematics: one yesterday, say a hundred today, about ten thousand tomorrow? He goes out of the lounge, the salty taste of the fish patties fouling his mouth, and retreats to the apartment to look out the window at the empty streets, patrolled from the air by the copters. Occasionally a soldier passes, dressed in a glittering plastic uniform and a plexiglass bubble helmet, his rifle slung on his shoulder and his other sanitation equipment dangling from his belt.

Dave has three options: scale the wire and try the Complex again, but inside that tunnel they will have the alternative of gassing him. The next is to scale the wire and try to get back to the outside, the middle ring, where he might be safe. The last is to wait it out, to see if the break will pass, but he suspects his chances are dim if he hangs around. The others too. They are through with options. He saw earlier on their faces the unmistakeable look of reckless desperation, and it seemed most evident in the girls, who were drinking pilfered wine and smoking marijuana. They would soon be dangerous to be near. They had been fearing this day for a long time, and the recklessness is easy to accept, like down-shifting on a hill before you need to. And the same recklessness is the next step for him if he fails to keep thinking of avoiding the germ. Had he known he would do all he had done the moment he walked through the Hudson Gate, he probably would have turned and gone north again. Degree by degree he had sunk into it, had wallowed, immersed himself in the germridden flesh of other humans to the point that the only surprise is that he still lives. And the death of fifty six today are beginning to make him snort. Who the hell cares any more? What difference does it make? Let's die and get it over with.

Recklessness is increasingly tantalizing.

It is almost as if some unseen hand wants to have this attitude tested: he must stand and think in order to recall the name of the girl who knocks and then slips into his place. At first he wonders if she is sick, but notices that she is drunk and high, so high in fact that she is almost incoherent. She stands reeling at the door. "Thought the bes' place to be would be with you," she says. "E'rybo'y's hero—Heee—ro!" she says, and staggers to the couch and flops on it. " 'r all gonna eat it today," she says, "all 'cept you, cause you're an *animal*! 'swat ol' Kellner—"

"Why don't you go to your place and go to sleep. In a few days it'll all be fine."

"Fine hell. We'll all be puking in a few days honey. 'way, Kellner says you're an animal," and she giggles, flopping back, her arms out. "Animal, on'y one here who's got a chance, a snowball's chance in a blast furnace, a mouse's chance in a cat house, 'see, other ones I forgot. Chinaman's chance in a—" She waves her hand at him and then tries to sit up. Then she flings her hands to her face and begins to laugh and cry at the same time in a sort of breathless whimper. He is embarrassed and goes and closes the door.

She struggles to her feet again, her face streaked and her breath coming in sobs. She looks angry now, and begins to reel toward the door, too drunk to make it. He helps her back to the couch, and the idiocy of it, the hopelessness that has suffused his and everyone else's spirit is just enough to make him fall over the line. He does not care any more. He pushes her back down on the couch.

It is as if he sees himself on a bright screen from some distance: consider this picture. Outside his window a helicopter passes in pursuit of another victim, who, robbed of his reason, will stagger in the streets until the machine descends to spray the gasses which will fry the lungs from the inside. In the apartment, intensely aware of the infliction of death outside and in fact made to feel a security that comes with the old familiarity (yes, this is the norm, the way it always was, the only difference being that here it is gas and liquid fire rather than bullets and wood fire), he experiences the powerful sense of comic despair and understands that there is nothing to stop him, not even her, who lies blearily gazing at him through her alcoholic mist. The desire to abandon himself is potently magnetic—he unbuckles the belt and pulls off her jeans, until they are inside out, the jeans wearing the underpants, and laughing, flings them behind him. Then he unzips the top so as to have at his disposal the complete expanse of nakedness. Not as hefty as Barbara by any stretch, but there she is: slight of build and pale, snickering at him with a strange light of understanding suddenly crossing her bloodshot eyes. She looks up at him with a penetrating look of dirty complicity, and he laughs, picks up her knees and spreads out her legs, so that under him in the glassy daylight is the vertical furrow just pinkly visible in the hair. Behind him is the flapflapflapflopflop of the copter seeking out its prey. In the air about his nostrils is the powerful vapor of a billion years of the history of the near extinct warm blooded animal. She drags him up over her body by his hair, her eyes closed and her face contorted with pleasure. Again he is amazed by the appropriateness of human anatomy. Ironic: there is still order in the universe. This is the urge that brought all those animals together to leave them victims of the Ceph, and it is the only thing left which might save them from their own extinction. These anatomical magnets: death's invitation and at the same time equipment of warm blooded desire and its result, continuation of the species. Why not? Might as well use it before it becomes dust.

Later she sleeps under his jacket, first proclaiming that she loves the smell of woodsmoke and skin grease. He stands at the window and watches the copters patrol. The Complex blocks his view of all but wafts of smoke and glints of windows in the middle distance. A mausoleum. Maybe Kellner was right—a magnet which gathered them all around itself so they could infect each other. He is not sure why, but now he knows he has to get out. But caught in the growing epidemic, he is not sure how to escape, or to where? Back to Buffalo? Or maybe to the sea? And what the hell should he look for? Out there, in any direction he chooses, there are only webbed skeletons, new clothes, gasless cars.

He goes downstairs to find Kellner. Only four people are there, two sitting across from each other in the large room, and two standing at a window pointing up in the direction of the Complex. Dave places himself at the greatest possible distance from them. "Where's Mr. Kellner?"

"Don't know," one says. "Upstairs trying to do what we're trying to do here? Figure out what to do? Pray? Who the hell knows?"

"What are you going to do?"

"What else? Get drunk."

The guy at the window turns. "Hey, you were up there. Maybe you could explain this?"

"What?" He points. Dave walks to a neutral window and searches the profile of the Complex, and up above the encircling nape, past the closer smoke, he sees something odd materialize in his vision—it looks as if darker smoke is pouring from three of the huge portholes on the side of the structure.

"Smokestacks?" the guy asks.

"No, looks like some kind of a fire or something." He squints. Below the smoke trailing up the side of the structure, he can see a tiny object, which he realizes in five seconds is a crashed helicopter lying below the burning portholes. It looks absurdly small, like a crushed spider, its propeller bent into an angular and twisted X over the wreckage of the cockpit. "Something must be wrong—some kind of explosion or something."

"Never seen anything like that before," the guy says.

"Must be some accident."

As the two at the window continue to speculate, Dave leaves and walks through halls pungent with spray disinfectant. Kellner's apartment door is closed. As Dave approaches, he feels a strange insecurity, as if something is out of place. He knocks. "Don't open it, don't open it!" Kellner shouts.

"It's me Dave." He waits, hears Kellner laugh.

It is the Ceph. Dave stands there looking at the blank door, and with a suddenly inexplicable force of its own, the fear invades him, and he trembles, smells immediately the stench of his fear rise around his face. "What? What's the matter? What's wrong?"

"I got it," Kellner says.

"No. What are the symptoms?"

"Clear as day," he says. "I'm not a novice at this, boy. Don't open the door. I got shakes, bad stomach, burning eyes, claustrophobia. Just leave the door closed."

Dave's heart thumps heavily and his mouth fills with the taste of copper. The Ceph can always hand him another surprise when he least expects it. Even now when the germ runs rampant, Kellner's eating it, Kellner, who had lasted so long, who had walked across the continent, grey hair and all, his eating it is a shock.

"You got to get out," Kellner says. "Listen, get out. Forget the Complex. It's a mistake."

"I already decided. I'm gonna go tonight," Dave says to the door.

"Tomorrow they'll gas the sector," Kellner says.

"The crazy ones'll get it in the streets, the okay ones inside'll be okay. Then each day, another spray."

"Is it all over? Everywhere?"

"We have no way of knowing. If there's a break-out, they stop the passage of information so the ones in the bad sectors won't try to break into the good ones. We won't know till it's over. Aha hahahaha! *You* won't know. Me? Hell, I'm forty seven. Wanted to retire in the Complex. Good food, pretty girls, all that. Guess now I'll retire under a pile of white powder. Hahaha!"

"Is there anything I can do?"

"No, I got me some good booze here, and a good view of the developments. Can even see some kind of a fire or something up in the Complex. Only thing is I don't have any way to end it when it gets too bad. I think I'm gonna do a swan dive off the porch. Would that do it?"

"Four stories? Head first? Sure."

And Kellner is almost whispering, as if he is talking to himself: "Kid, you know what my last thought will be? I'll see you off in the woods somewhere, getting old on good books and booze. Listen, consider yourself your father's contribution to the species. He was a genius. I'll die okay, cause I know there's somebody else whose got the secret. Forget this place. It's a reduction of the old world into metaphor."

"What?"

"The bug *is* death. All it comes down to is how you use the time you got. We all made a mistake by coming here to wait for— For what? The promise of eternal life I guess. We all forgot we gotta die anyway. We weren't even really alive."

Dave laughs. "But what the hell's the point?"

"Of what? Of living? Invent one for chrissakes. People've been doing it for a million years." He groans, and Dave hears a piece of furniture fall over.

He backs up, looking at the door. "Oh christ I feel shitty," Kellner says. "Listen, get out soon. Sharpen your arrows and run. Head for the colder climates. As far as you can get. Adios tough guy. Better get out before the shit hits the fan. I'm getting drunk."

IV

Dave is preparing his gear. He counts his arrows: fourteen hunting, three target. He is amazed that the circumstances, as unpredictable as they were, still left him with this valuable equipment. He has been a fool for leaving them around. He gently runs his fingers along the bow string to make sure it is not frayed. In the dim light of a single candle, he goes over the mechanical parts of the bike, checking each link of the chain, the system of gears which looks like a conical silver flower, concentric circles of teeth out to the bolt in the middle. He has food pilfered from the kitchen downstairs: one gallon of distilled water, fifteen of the salty cakes containing the fish. He has kitchen utensils, a fair knife, matches.

Outside are the periodic noises of the Ceph's

progress and its spinoff: occasional shots indicate the passing of more victims, moans, maniacal laughs, screams from those victims not yet tracked down and executed. For them it is only a matter of time. The militarys, encased in their plastic uniforms and clear plexiglass bubble masks, lurk in the shadows, their weapons and flame throwers ready, their white powder, gasses, disinfectants dangling from their belts in small spray guns. The poor victim may walk into an alley, his eyes running and his reason ebbing quickly, and be shot, burned, gassed and disinfected all inside of five seconds. Dave must make his way out by getting past the militarys and their equally dangerous prey, and the militarys are on orders to eliminate anyone who is not honoring the curfew or anyone who tries to get through the wire enclosing the doomed sector. He will have to scuttle the bike on the way because he will not be able to get it through the billows of wire. He prepares it anyway because it may be necessary to race for the wire if he is seen. If he waits till dawn he is a goner, because by then the sector will be aflame with clouds of the bug, which will radiate from new victims escaping into the streets. The helicopters will have to gas the whole place. The geometric process, the progression, seems to him too quickly mounting to permit him to stay another day. Tomorrow the new victims will rise from their fitful sleep and may not be sure until they are outside on their porches, where the sunlight will seem harsh, the very flesh will seem uncomfortable, so that the touch of anything will be unpleasant.

He believes it is around four o'clock. He is not scared, nor is he uncertain or tired. It is simply time to go. The last report on Kellner sucked all emotion from him. Someone saw, around eleven at night, the form hurtling down from an upper story. The man at the window had been speculating on the absence of lights on part of the Complex—a roughly diamond shaped space of blackness against the blinking lights. About halfway up the stacks. Blackout? Power failure due to—what? And then the form hurtling to the ground. Then Kellner sat up, stunned at the failure of his own suicide, and watched the soldiers descend on him. He apparently laughed as the fire arced out into his face.

Dave passed by the lounge with his pilfered food as they cringed and backed off and held their faces. Now, with Kellner gone and death a near certainty, the prospect of trying to get out seems like motion without meaning. What the hell is there beyond the wire? More victims, and beyond that, away from the Complex, oh yes he knows: he figured it out. His trip from Buffalo went seven hundred kilometers, like a piece of thread over the state. Beyond that fence, he could travel back and forth across the continent a thousand times, each time paralleling his previous thread by only two or three hundred meters. He could spend a hundred lives doing this, and all he would ever find would be desolation, so complete, so universal that it dulls his mind, and he does not know why he is leaving and he does not care.

He sees again, in the profound silence of that winter house of six or eight years ago, the graceful arc of the blue vase he threw and the resulting shattering of the silence as it hit the television screen. He will make it back to that desolation to fulfill what may be his purpose on earth, to make noise. For the present, that will have to sustain him.

He strings the bow. He looks out into the clear night. The Complex twinkles, minus that one space halfway up. A breakout of the bug maybe. It makes no difference. Nearer, here and there the military's fires make orange forms dance on building sides. The occasional sounds of violence continue. Ironically, the air seems cool, indicating that the heat wave might be passing. Charlie's looseleaf book of instructions sits safely in the knapsack, and when he puts it on he feels the book's form against his back. He is ready.

He makes his way slowly, from alley to alley and house to house in the motionless predawn blackness. Once his eyes are used to the darkness, they can perceive shapes, lighter planes of color. He carries the bike on his shoulder because if run along the sidewalks it would make soft clicks inside the bearing housing. Absolute silence is necessary. He knows that the militarys wait in secret places, their gasses ready. And the Ceph-ridden victims also hide from the militarys, having been ousted from their places by neighbors, or in the later stages, stumbling out in partial madness, finding the close quarters of rooms unbearable. It is only a matter of time before they give themselves away with moans, hopeless laughs, telltale sounds that come with the retching and the other last stages. They know they must die, but are afraid of the methods employed by the militarys, who will shoot and gas at such speed that the dying, perhaps grateful for the single sting of the bullet, may find themselves shocked that they do not die quickly enough to avoid having their lungs fried. Kellner had observed this, he had said. "You know, smoke comes out of their mouths? They lie there after taking one breath and smoke comes out of their mouths?"

Dave does not know where he goes exactly. He travels with his back to the Complex, figuring that the sector fence cannot be more than a few hundred meters away.

Something halts him. Ahead there is the dim suggestion of street, more buildings, but under that, on the sidewalk, a shape. He darts his eyes around the shape to give it definition, and it materializes slowly as a man sitting, head bowed. Then the man coughs, groans, mutters a garbled curse at his own gesturing hand. If he yells, then the militarys will be drawn to him. If he gets up and moves, wafts of deadly air will boil off him. Dave's eyes continue to experience the picture, and the man achieves greater definition. He will make noise soon. Dave swallows, feels his legs weaken. He must kill the man as silently as possible before he screams or vomits. Being perfectly practical and objective about it, he *should* kill him. The total absence of near light means that the militarys are off somewhere else executing, but a scream would draw them. But with the strange, ticklish sensation rising in his chest he cannot avoid the feeling that he is up to something dirty and experimental.

He moves so slowly that he is almost not moving. The bike leans lightly against the brick wall. The arm goes up over the shoulder, and the forefinger, experienced, runs over the rear tips of the arrows in search of one of the target ones, which he will send into the man's temple. The sound will be a pop, hopefully not enough to draw any attention. The twang will be worse, since there is a high, almost metallic ring to it, but he will take the chance. His hands shake as he roots the arrow. He approaches, drawing it back. The man mutters again, this time louder, and then comes out with a hoarse sob.

A powerful shaft of light sweeps the sky above him. Militarys. It disappears, and Dave can tell only that its source is ahead of him toward the fence. Now, he draws, aims and lets off. The string whips his wrist and there is a powerful scream, and then up the street, the sound of the arrow shaft bouncing. Dave grabs the bike and retreats on rubber legs and the man screams again, at which three beams of light scan the street. Dave's wrist burns and itches—a stupid mistake. He is hot with shame. Only amateurs do that. The arrow apparently ricocheted off the man's head, trenching it on the way. Dave finds an alley, parks the bike and roots another arrow, waiting. The white spots materialize down the street and approach the man, who holds his bleeding head. Two spots stop, trained on him. The third approaches to within five meters and then comes the shot. The dying man's head snaps against the wall and he slumps forward on his face. The soldier approaches closer and suddenly the street is almost as bright as day. The flame engulfs the body, which continues to burn after the flame retreats dribbling into the thrower. At the end of the burning arc small droplets of fire bounce on the street in a dotted line. Then the device is extinguished, and the soldier approaches again, glittering in the light from the other spots, and sends a spray of white dust on the burning body. The fire goes out, and he continues to spray until the dust, which foams on contact, leaves only the suggestion of the shape of the dead man. The soldiers leave.

He stands in the alley for five minutes, his eyes constructing phantom fires before him. Behind the imagined fire there is blackness, and until his eyes adjust he must wait. When they begin again to perceive shapes, he realizes that the sky is lightening now. Dawn is on the way, and he must hurry. The fact of having missed the man's head has undermined his feeling of direction, if he had any to begin with. Now he feels like a deranged and aimless animal, hurtling itself for no reason into a vast, abysmal blackness.

There was a saying for it: the frying pan into the fire. Something Charlie used to say. He knew, chuckling hopelessly and coming to a sliding stop and seeing the dying man on the wire, he understood why the soldier had called him an asshole and why, in the early morning light, squirming through the wire, he was not regarded as any threat to anybody. Sitting in an alley and looking back at the wire-billowed no man's land he had just crossed, and looking at the soldiers in their plastic suits on the other side, he darted frightened glances around him and scanned the old sector perimeter for his bicycle.

He had to ditch it when he broke into a run, now with the bow folded and in the quiver. He traded the bike for a plank of light wood he found jammed into the foundation of an old house, trotted toward the wire, and then bellyflopped the board on the wire and skittered across, hearing behind him a hoarse laugh. "Asshole!" a guy yelled, and Dave ended up tangled in the last billow of wire, fought his way through it without a scratch with that tense and adrenalin juiced caution and found himself safe on the other side, panting and crawling backwards toward the nearest building, wondering why he was not being shot at by those in the new sector. Then by absurd chance a man, face blotched by tears and running out of balance, threw himself at the wire, just barely got to it when he was cut down by bullets, and then a plastic soldier from his old sector came to the wire and arced a stream of fire over the fence and deftly settled a bonfire on the poor victim who had made an attempt to escape his Ceph-ridden sector into a safe one.

This sector was worse than his own, far deeper into the progression of mass infection. He barely got his breath before he heard the ancient sounds of people finding solace in their misery: a scream, a maniacal laugh, glass breaking. Out came the bow and a hunting arrow. He hid in the back of the alley, trying to pull his senses together. Then a man came in from the street, dragging a woman behind him. She wore a faded dressing gown and swung at him wildly. "C'mon," he said, "what the hell difference— What the— An hour for chrissake, one goddam hour and it's all over. C'mon," and she fought on, and the man, already bleary eyed, struck her once across the head and rammed his hand inside the gown. She batted him on the head a couple times and he laughed hoarsely, working his hand at her. "Oh juicy lady!" he said. "C'mon." She began to relax in her exhaustion, her arms flopping limply. "There," he said, "there—" Then she noticed Dave and screamed and broke from the man and came down the alley. Dave raised and let off and hit her in the sternum with a loud pop and she fell on the rear of the arrow, sending it out through her back as she landed. The man stumbled back, wiping his sleeve across his mouth. The woman gurgled, raised her head and looked at Dave, gulped some blood out of her mouth and then let her face fall into it.

He left the alley by scaling a small fence at the back. Out to the street again. To his right was a man's corpse, lying in the attitude of sleep with his head lying in the vomit, the hair neatly combed. To the right, nothing, and he went along the wall, another arrow out. You must not let them get close. You must hit them sure before they get within fifteen feet. Something hit the street in front of him, sending up a little puff of grey smoke, and he heard the sound of the shot from the wire and backed into an open doorway. It was an apartment hallway. The first door he peeked into gave him a slice of a picture. He moved left and right and made out a man sitting with a bottle in his lap muttering and gazing with bleary bloodshot eyes at the wall. Drunk or sick, no way to tell.

He left, holding his breath, looking for a west-bound street. He would run the quarter mile across the sector and go through another fence. Hah! Fuck it, he would run through a thousand fences and a thousand doomed sectors, he would pop a million people, so what? He would execute, execute, execute, until his goddamned arm got tired, till he was up to his knees in blood, until he got so bored that he would drop his weary bow and find some Ceph-ridden young piece of meat and die happy, all teary eyed and humping away like mad. Who the hell ever needed balance lying down? If he made it with his life he would become a punk and devote his life to their cause: sneaking in sharp eyed hellraising, miner sacking and pussy hunting on the perimeter of this sinkhole of death. Execute! A corpse a day keeps the Ceph away. Avoid death by becoming its agent. That's what they all did, the punks, militarys. Brilliant—don't run from those with the bug. Track them down and kill them before they die.

Did this sense of freedom ever make him brave—he strolled around a corner, bow in hand, and scanned the street. Here and there a body, off in the distance staggering forms: a woman, a little older, seemingly feeling her way along. Two men stumbling in different directions, unaware of each other. And the sounds: screams, oh yes, the last agony, Jesus is it horrible to hate the sensation of your own flesh so much that you would just go mad feeling that exposed nerve from the eyes down, the quivering jaw, the fumbling hands, the weird sensation of wanting to figure out how to throw your guts out of your mouth and into the street. He knew that sooner or later he would have to go through just that, but he would not be a fool, he would find a way to avoid it.

No one disturbed him as he walked. It was still only about six o'clock, and those not yet maddened were still pacing their rooms or peering fearfully from their windows. Militarys probably were on the perimeter. If he saw one he would kill him. Why not? We're all in this game together.

With the increasing light the doomed continued to emerge from buildings. As he remembered from New Florence, the powerful impulse to escape the condition of being locked in a body aflame with the advancing nervous itch, the searing tickle, would make the people break into a stumbling run looking for an avenue of escape, and the beginning heat of morning aggravated it, light itself pushed the impulse to frenzy. Dave hid in an alley between two buildings, and the narrow strip of vision of the street showed him the people stumbling by in both directions. He held the bow at half cock, calmly prepared to kill the first person to enter the alley.

The militarys had apparently been waiting for the people to come out too. From above he heard the distant flopping of helicopters, and suddenly understood—gas. Up and down the streets they would go, spewing the stuff all around. Kellner explained it to him. Those not yet pushed to the last degree of madness would keep themselves sealed in their houses until the raid was over, and thus put off death for a while. The healthy would stay in too. The gassing process would be repeated once or twice a day for a week, and in this way all the sick would eventually be eliminated, leaving legitimate survivors and maybe a few extra fugitives from execution. He had to find shelter.

Out on the street again. The screams were louder, the bustle of mass desperation came across in a mingling of sounds: the increasing flapflapflap-flopfloptuptup of the approaching copters, the sounds of nails being driven and doors and windows being slammed, the closer sounds of laughs, moans, screams and retching. Holding the bow at half cock he worked his way along the street looking for a door, all the time trying to keep his distance from those stumbling along, some walking dazed, some crawling, here a mother staggering doggedly pursued by her screaming child, there a man lying on the macadam on his back laughing at the sky. Some stood with shocked faces while the contents of stomachs shot through fingers gripped over mouths, others acknowledged that powerful impulse and bent over and threw up.

Across the street on a corner he saw a bald man in a sleeveless tee shirt run out on a lawn and grab a little girl, intending to pull her inside. He did so, and then appeared in a window, hammering. Dave took the chance. The first helicopter came into view up the street, sweeping low over the macadam, the billows of gas expanding behind it. Those only briefly engulfed were driven back as if hit in the face by something heavy, and fell in a backward arch so that the head hit the pavement first. Dave ran across the front lawn, up the steps and slammed into the as yet unlocked door and found himself in the living room, bow full drawn, finger gently hooked, aiming at the man's chest. The woman screamed, the girl hid behind her.

"I swear I'll kill you—you got to let me stay."

"You fucking—"

"Close the door, the copter's here. C'mon." The man went, sweating and glancing fearfully behind him. Then he slammed two four by four beams into lock brackets.

"Stay away," the man said. To his wife he said, "go upstairs, don't come down." They went up. "Fuckin' bastards," he said, "out every goddam night passin' bottles around, fuckin' dirty whores, tradin' worthless shit. It's your fault."

"Go over there, to the other side. One move and I'll split your belly."

"Big deal," he said, waving his hand at Dave, "you goddamned punks, think you got the world by the tail just cause you got a little bow and arrow. Put that down and I'll break your goddam head, 'cept I'd get the bug too, like you."

"I ain't got it. I got nothin'. I'm tryin' to get out."

"Sure," he said, and continued talking as the

copter went by. Dave peeked out. The gas, like a mist, billowed across the lawn. "These windows tight?"

"No," the man whined sarcastically, "I never bothered. Never occurred to me to make them tight."

"I was just askin'."

A back window broke. Dave ran to the hall. Across the kitchen a red eyed man was trying to climb in. He raised and let off in a quick motion and splattered the base of the man's throat. The bald man appeared behind him as he loaded again. He gestured to Dave to move, aimed a spray can into the kitchen, filled it with mist and shut the door.

"Air's so shitty now they'll look somewhere else."

"Yeah, gas is creepin' around there too."

The man laughed. "What a world. What a fuckin' circus."

"You said a mouthful."

"Well, you stay on that side of the room and I'll stay here. Keep that bow loaded too. I guess since you got rid of that looney there— Well, stay. Gas's toxic element'll be gone in an hour."

"Thanks, I hadda do somethin'. All the empty places got maggot food inside."

"Hahahaha! Maggot food. A card, a real card. Say, smell that?"

"Yeah, sweet, kinda."

"That's what kills ya. I was in one of these a couple years ago, in Union City."

"No kidding?"

"That's right. Same smell, but we're getting about one percent of what the poor loonies out there get. They're dead already. I tell you, it's God's punishment, that's what."

They waited. After a while they stood at different windows to speculate on the meaning of the black smoke stains above the portholes which burned yesterday. "Neighbor of mine says there was an outbreak in there. Says they're no better off than we are. The food's the thing that worries me, though." Dave looked. The smoke stains were only small tongues of black on the monstrous form, which he saw now looming off at the end of a street littered with bodies.

He did not want to impose on the man longer than an hour, because he was afraid that he may have had the Ceph. He thanked him, adjusted his knapsack and left, setting his back to the Complex, and slowly made his way along a street toward the border of the sector, aware that the field militarys would be out seeking stragglers. The absence of any movement indicated the success of the gassing operation. Inside of one minute, the progress of one block, he became aware of the forms behind him, glittering in the distance dusting the corpses, their round plexiglass masks glinting in the sun. The militarys swept from the east, and Dave, looking for the fence, would gradually be hemmed in. He walked on. Ahead two hundred meters was the border, in this case a divided highway suspended over the ground with billows of wire strung from pillar to pillar. It was not merely a sector border. The depth of the billows of wire told him that it was the border of the inner ring. Yes, atop the wire, on the highway, he saw the moving forms, the heavier firepower protecting the legitimate subordinate population from the illegitimate on the outside. The border would be so deep that crossing it would be impossible. He turned, saw the glittering forms enlarging in the growing heat. They encircled a straggler, shot him, descended with their equipment. Another straggler came out of an alley, saw them, and stumbled back in.

It was a simple process of the reduction of possibilities: as the morning wore on, he found himself working in a smaller belt of safety, cautiously and calmly paralleling the inner ring border in a broad zigzag, seeing with each dip back toward the Complex the glittering militarys at their business, now large enough in his vision to see clearly. And each experimental movement to the highway which gradually swept downward to the earth resulted in the clearer forms of the soldiers patrolling the border.

When he saw his only possible escape he chuckled and shook the sweat from his face. Across the street was a boarded up auto tunnel, over which was an old illegible sign, and under the sign in bold and hasty block letters was written: "Disposal—Do Not Enter. Tunnel Blocked." There was no way of telling how long it had been since the tunnel was used for disposal. There was no way of knowing what was on the other end. If it dipped, as he suspected it did, then it was likely to be flooded. He sat on his haunches and waited, his mind ticking off the old cautions: *avoid enclosures, barns, where manure, no matter how old, is piled.* Another he remembered vaguely had to do with damp air and its hazards. Half of the problem depended on how old the corpses were. If they were skeletons, he was all right. If there was water in the tunnel, then he was in trouble.

He rose, loped slowly across the street and to the boarded up tunnel. Its ceiling was arched, perhaps twenty feet high. Through a chink in the boards he saw the rear ends of heavily dusted cars with flat tires. He pulled a board off and squeezed through and immediately smelled the funky scent of ancient death. Not bad, almost like a swamp. He was in luck. The system of disposal was to coast the cars out to the streets, put the bodies inside, then return them to the tunnel. He sat inside and looked back, saw the plastic soldiers coming out of the alleys and streets, waving to the men on the elevated highway. Some of the soldiers were picked up by little squat electric trucks, which pulled trailers behind them. Once they were gone, Dave opened his knapsack to look for the candle and matches.

"Fox in the hole," he heard. Soldiers. They saw him. He rose, his bow ready, grabbed the knapsack, turned and began running between the cars. In the middle distance he saw that the cars faced the exit, which meant that the end of the disposal part was there. "Hey! Fox in the hole!" He ran deeper into the blackness.

He came aware lying on his back, blearily gazing at the ceiling. His head throbbed and his voice came to him in distant moans.

Sarge fox in the hole, bring up the throwers. Can't see him. Back a ways. Permission to go in.

Gimme that fucker.

The ceiling was ablaze with light. Dave tried to roll over. His right eye burned. He lifted his hand to it and came away with blood. How? Trying to focus, he saw the open rear door of a station wagon, its sharp metal corner just at head level.

Go on in and get him then.

Hey, hey bring the gas. Get me the gas. Who's got the gas?

Dave groped for the bow, groaning, gasping for breath, dizzy and nauseated. His right eye was okay. The blood ran into it and blinded him. He did not touch the cut. The bow and quiver were ahead. Then the ceiling was ablaze with light again, and he felt intense heat. They were settling bonfires a carlength away, trying to burn him. They sprayed gas in, trying to get the slow billows to reach him.

Go get him then. Get on in there.

He has a bow.

Dave tried to stand, but couldn't. He crawled deeper into the tunnel, moaning, his head searing with pain. Through his flooding eyes he tried to watch himself root an arrow. Then he dropped it. He turned, saw the form working its way through the hole in the entrance. Dave groped for the arrow, looked up and saw the hunched form coming in, the nozzle of his hose dripping fire. The drops of fire made a dotted line.

I got him. Got him on his knees.

Drop the fucker.

The form hunched. Dave was on his knees, feeling the macadam for the arrow, his eyes blinded by the blood. He saw the silhouette enlarge, the nozzle spurt briefly and continue to drip. He was almost too exhausted to try.

There, the familiar shaft. Onto the string it went. In an agonized rush of energy he set, hooked the finger and let off. The squirt of fire drenched the wall, and the cave was as bright as day. The soldier screamed, the arrow in his chest, and fell back. The echo ran up and down the tunnel as the soldier fell, the nozzle now on the macadam and leaking a little river of fire. Dave grabbed the gear and stumbled deeper into the tunnel, hearing behind him the soldiers yelling.

He heated the spoon over a candle. Using a mirror kicked off a car, he saw that he had a two inch laceration on his forehead, which had to be treated. First, he took the hot spoon, and holding the mirror, rolled it once over the cut, sizzling the flesh, and choked off a scream by gripping his mouth with trembling hands dripping with sweat. When the impulse to scream was gone he was cold with his sweat, and sobbed with each breath. But softly. He was afraid the soldiers might have followed him. His nose ran, his ears rang with the pain. Now. He took the piece of flat metal with the large pool of blood on it and held it over the candle and watched the blood turn brick red as it gradually dried. The close concentration on holding it kept him from feeling too much pain. When the blood was dry enough he slowly and clumsily pulverized it with the spoon's rounded back. He put the powder into the spoon, pinched the now numb laceration shut, made it bleed a little, and then jammed the full spoon on the cut. He made a bandanna out of the sleeve of his shirt, wrapped it around his head, and tightened it over a squared wad of shirtsleeve and tied it tightly in place. When he stood he felt dizzy, and his head throbbed with pressure. He put his knapsack on. He felt barely alive, an organism moving only by reflex. He held the candle high, and the shadows moved on the walls of the tunnel with the movement of his hand. He thought, fuck it. His will had become a sullen force, almost unconscious. He would go on. A bug stepped on and dragging its quick behind it, mangled all to hell, still moved on.

The journey through the first third of the tunnel amounted to jumping from car to car, up to the roof, down onto the trunk, over the hood, up onto the roof. There was not enough room between them. He did it slowly, with extreme care, blurting out curses whenever he jarred his body enough to have the electric zap of pain hit his head. In the middle somewhere he had to scale two semi trucks, had to crawl over the roofs rather than walk because their tops were too close to the tunnel ceiling. The tunnel did dip as he had expected, and with each car, the level of the black water rose closer and closer to the hoods and rear trunks. Each time he landed on a car he created a small, glittering system of concentric circles of ripples. He held the candle high and saw the dotted line of cartops go down and into the black water. There were no mosquitoes in the tunnel, meaning that the water had oil on it or was poisoned.

The only way to go on would be to work along the thick encased wire bolted to the side of the tunnel. You should not get wet, he thought. He had never been swimming in his life. Immersion in water used to mean death. "Shit," he said, and the "it it it it" sound reverberated up and down the tunnel. Touching another human meant death too. He tightened the straps of his knapsack so that it sat high on his back. In order to insure that there would be no problem transferring himself from the car to the wire, he slowly let himself off the side of the one he stood on, feeling the rank and awful coldness run up his legs as the water seeped through his jeans. He held the candle high, noticing that the wire was too high yet to reach, so he made his way slowly along, suddenly experiencing for the first time in his life the sensation of buoyancy, which startled him. He climbed back up on a fender and his mouth filled with the taste of copper and the rancid smell of fear rose into his nostrils. He began to breathe very deeply and hard, staring at the black water. It was the feeling of buoyancy which robbed him of control of movement, his feet superficially searching the ground for stability, which was horrible. He sat on the fender, his legs in the water, trying to convince himself that people used to swim, that it was common, even fun.

The rotten pounding in his head drove him back in. He climbed along the sides of the cars slowly, going for radio antennas, door handles, until they were too far under, and the wire was finally accessable. The buoyancy, he found, was an advantage. Once on the wire he was so far out of the water that he felt as heavy as lead, and holding it with one hand and the candle with the other was impossible. He put the candle butt into the crook of his elbow, so that he could grip the wire with the same arm that held the candle. The further he worked his way along, the lighter he became, until, when the water was up to the top of his stomach, it was quite easy. The only uncomfortable point was when the hot wax dripped into his one remaining shirtsleeve and burned his arm.

In the blackness there seemed to be no time. He worked, rested, hung on the wire and closed his eyes, the coldness making him tremble. His fingers became numb, he let the lower part of his body wave in the water like a rag. Then he would start again, slowly sliding along the wire, his head reactivating its throbbing. Gradually it became more difficult to move, which meant that he was going up again. He looked ahead. Out in the distant limits of his vision he saw again the cartops emerging from the water. So. He made it.

The sullen recognition made him stop, think, look down at the black water and his own warped reflection rippling in the expanding rings of little waves. He began to breathe faster, and then it was as if he could not breathe at all. He almost messed his pants. With the increase in the possibility of making it, so came the hated workings of his imagination: they were all here. She is here. His mother, faded dress, bloodshot eyes, lusting wide-eyed for one of the fugitives—escaped it again!

He worked along the wire, juiced by his fear, muttering, goggle-eyed: the dead, angry, tear at their own pale and nerveless skin, lacerating it with anguish that he who had made so many mistakes, should again escape. They are rising from the water, groping slowly, they want to wrench his viscera from him since it fails to rise into his insolent mouth. They move under the water like mindless fish, strings of mucous waving lazily from the corners of their mouths. They reach, only a foot, only inches from gripping his numbed ankle.

When he reached the other end of the tunnel, which was blocked by dirt and rubble and had only a small wired up opening at the top, he was exhausted and hungry and frightened.

The chink through which he would squirm to freedom: he could see that it was dark outside, and in the distance were the old sounds: the shouting, laughing, breaking of bottles on macadam. Yes, this was it, the middle ring, and in those sounds he heard a familiar tone: those people breaking bottles and beating each other up and sacking old men and looking for girls to gang rape in garbage strewn alleys were not sick, they were merely raising holy hell in a place free from the Ceph.

He stalks the streets, passing among the little groups of thugs and the staggering and hopeless drunks and the whores who lurk near streetcorner fires. They are all interested in what he carries in the bag on his shoulders, but the halfdrawn bow holds their curiosity in check. His drying clothes stink, and one man notes this: "Oooeee! Where you been chief?"

"Nowhere."

"What you got in the bag?"

"Come on over and find out."

"There's more than one of us here sonny."

"I'm the one who figures out who gets split first. Come ahead fuckface."

"Now now, come have a little wine."

"Nah, I'm on my way."

He will find a bike, steal one. He walks, the bow half cocked, keeping himself in open space. Behind him in the sky is the massive, twinkling Complex with that one space of blackness.

"Hey Robin Hood. Where you going?"

"Acapulco."

"Want to put a little honey on your stinger, sugar?"

"Not tonight lady."

"Too bad, cause I got lots of honey tonight."

"Yeah, well—"

"Bye-bye," she says. "Don't let your meat loaf."

The bike: two nice ten speeders are left unattended by two men who are bargaining with a drunken woman at the back of an alley. In the dim firelight he sees them feeling her up and pleading like children. Dave hikes the nicest one on his shoulder so it will not make noise.

He streaks along the macadam in the approaching dawn surprising groups of thugs and getting beyond them before they can even think of sacking him. He is exhilarated by the sensation of a good bike clicking away between his legs. He rides for an hour, grinning into the wind which presses his eyes. Into Punk country, past a couple of dozing border guards who say nothing as he passes. The familiar desolation brightens in the sunrise.

The bow full drawn, he aims at the chest of the boy. He is about thirteen, ragged, shocked at the failure of his wire stretched across the road. "Please don't," he whines, "we din' mean—"

"Others? Get them out here. Now."

They emerge from behind trees, old rubble. There are nine in all. Half are girls. All are younger than the punk who tried to sack him, except for one girl, who is perhaps thirteen. Straining against her black imitation leather, sequin studded jacket are two lumps. She wears leather jeans and furlined boots. All are dressed in pilfered clothes. They prefer bright studs, Indian headbands, thick belts with brass buckles and gaudy, sequined jackets. They look ridiculous.

"What the hell is this?" Dave asks, releasing to half cock.

The boy looks hungrily at his knapsack. It is clear that they are all hungry, frothing at the mouth for something to eat. "There's a couple more little ones in the bushes. Dying."

"Lemme see."

They lie, sunken eyes and fat bellies, dying of starvation, looking up at him with wan curiosity. "They're done for."

"We din' wanna kill them. My cousins, both. The rest are from other families. We all got something, like stomach flu or something, and they put us in a wagon and left us out here."

"What did you do for food?"

They all laugh. "We ate weeds, flowers, stuff we dug up, any old stuff we could find."

Dave looks back toward the Complex, then at the road. "Yeah, food's hard to get around here. You gotta go way out." His head throbs again. He should be off, but suddenly, in the morning heat, he is tired. He sighs. "Well, c'mere," and he distributes to them one cake apiece, which they wolf down before he even notices they take it. "Now, drink water, but find your own cups." They disappear, emerge from the bushes with old coffeestained styrofoam cups, chipped mugs. He fills each glass and cup and watches them drink.

"Your head's bleeding," the boy says.

"It's okay. When you guys ate all this junk you dug up, did any of you croak of the Ceph?"

"Nope."

"How long you been here?"

"Two or three weeks?"

"Did you boil your water?"

"Sometimes."

"Idiots," he says, "it's a wonder you're alive." They all laugh appreciatively.

He tells them part of his story, tells them that there is no percentage staying around here, that they should all either try to get back in or go away, far away. As he talks he looks frequently at the oldest girl. She isn't too skinny, and has nice meat around the hips. She is dirty, with knots of curly blonde hair and blackened nails. She has good teeth.

Finally he says, "you're all crazy. You got no notion of how to live. Look at you. You look awful." They look down. "I'm takin' her with me."

"Who, her?"

"Yeah, who do you think?"

"Aw, come on," the older boy says, "mister, don't. Sides, she isn't old enough to do it yet."

"You shut your goddamned mouth," she yells. "You shut up. How the fuck do you know anything? Who the hell are you?"

"Well I was just—"

"Well you keep your goddam mouth shut!" she yells, her arms folded, "how the hell do you know anything about girls?"

"Okay okay, I was just—"

"Then shut up. One word and I'll knock you on your ass!"

"Jesus!" Dave says, "quiet, my head!"

One day Dave woke up and peeked out of his sleeping bag, and his eye was on the white painted edge of the dotted line which runs down the middle of one of the eight lanes of route ninety. It had rained a little. He checked the healing sore on his head, and sat up. The sun was coming up over the trees, and he gazed at the immense strip of highway which disappeared into the western horizon, which was still the dark blue black of early morning. As he rose from the bag he rubbed his eyes and looked back. Goddamned slowpokes. He couldn't get anywhere with them hanging on. He had told them that they must never be out of sight of the highway. It was his job to zigzag into the country in search of old wheat, old gardens, good water. If he wanted to attract their attention he set fire to a barn or house. They now obeyed without argument. Today they would catch up with him, struggling along on their kids' bikes, pulling their wagonloads of garbage, their sick, one of whom died three days out and the other, a little girl, who seemed to be getting better.

On the same day the child died, in fact just as they were throwing handfuls of dirt down on the blanketed form, the ground began to tremble in a long, softly rumbling vibration. They stood looking at it silently until the sick girl began to cry and the other smaller children began running around screaming with excitement about earthquakes, the earth splitting and swallowing them up, volcanoes, the sun going out like a light. Then the vibration went away and they moved on. At night, just after dusk, the eastern sky stayed light, but a strange half circle of red light swept high into the sky, and it remained there throughout the night, brightest about two hours before the dawn consumed it and changed it later into a mountain of grey, probably smoke. Because Dave stayed away from the kids most of the time he let them do their own speculating about whether or not the complex was gone. Dave stayed sullen and numb about it, dully supposing that anything could be true, that he might as well figure the familiar map contour of the eastern part of the continent had probably heaved and split off and slid into the ocean.

At first the kids were noisy and raucous, and stayed that way after the tremor and the glow. They went around making little bows and arrows and shooting at each other as usual until the fourth day, when one little boy hit a little girl in the face with a crude arrow and broke the skin. It was probably because the tremor and the red glow meant there would now be no going back that Dave threw down what he was doing and started yelling at the boy—"you broke the skin, you made her just right for the germ!" The kid began to whimper, his finger in his nose. "And while I'm at it," Dave roared, "never pick your nose. Never!" By now he had them all listening. "The nose carries germs—leave it alone." He stopped, looked around. "Okay, goddammit, you listen now," and he lectured them for ten minutes—bows and arrows are only for target practice. There is no other use for it except to sharpen your aim. He took the remaining hunting arrows from his quiver, strung his bow, and sent them one by one in long, soaring arcs out onto the amber fields of grass. Then he continued, saying that the bow is only for whatchacallit, for practicing being fit and nothing else. In some town they'd go get some new ones, and everybody would learn to hit an apple at fifty feet. And everyone would learn to read or be left behind. Everyone would learn about health or be left behind. If they were going to follow him all over the goddamned countryside, then they would do as he said. After that, it was quiet for the rest of the day.

That night and the nights after when they finally caught up with signs he left on the highway, he called them over to the fire and sat them down around it and told them about what they had to know and where they were going. He would hold before him the little looseleaf book, tipping it into the flickering orange light, and read from it. Each night Rose, the oldest girl, would sit a little closer to him, filing her nails and looking frequently into her pocket mirror, sometimes pausing thoughtfully at some rule about health or food that Dave read.

This morning he rose to eat the milky seeds of wheat and made ready for a trip into the fields. Behind that there was something else sitting at the back of his mind, which he was almost afraid to acknowledge. He had made the halfconscious counting, and sitting on the highway this morning he realized that this was the morning of the eighth day since his escape from the inner ring, and the only symptom he felt was hunger, and thirst.

He looked at his hands, and at the foreshortened

view of his body, still afraid to figure out exactly what day it was, for fear that he might be wrong. But he knew he was right. My God, he thought, standing. Jesus God. Well, he was lucky, and he would not push it. The full degree of his sacrilege hit him. He had sinned, wallowed, tried to give up his life, and he would never never never do it again. They would go by the book. They would watch out for themselves. Rules would be rules. What the hell else was there? He chuckled. There was that other business: it excited the hell out of the little kids, so much that he was believing it himself. He had felt the necessity to provide a reason for all this, to invent some justification, so he told them, speaking into the fire, that birds lived somewhere, and one of the things that they were doing and must never forget, was that one of the places they looked for, thousands of miles away across the whole continent, was supposed to have birds, and he told them many times what to look for, what to listen for, that if it happened, if this tiny phantom of the past chose one day to reveal itself, it would be in a flash across the field of your vision, like a thrown stone in a peculiar trajectory that you knew defied gravity, a process of self-sustained flight that was absolutely unmistakable once you saw it.

MS READ-a-thon—a simple way to start youngsters reading

Boys and girls between 6 and 14 can join the MS READ-a-thon and help find a cure for Multiple Sclerosis by reading books. And they get two rewards—the enjoyment of reading, and the great feeling that comes from helping others.

Parents and educators: For complete information call your local MS chapter. Or mail the coupon below.

Kids can help, too!

Mail to:
National Multiple Sclerosis Society
205 East 42nd Street
New York, N.Y. 10017

I would like more information about the MS READ-a-thon and how it can work in my area.

Name ______________________________
(please print)

Address ______________________________

City ______________ State ________ Zip ________

Organization ______________ ______________

78JY